M. J. Boyle was born in the mid-1950s in the North, grew up in the South of England but has spent her adult life in Europe. Her strong ties to her home country and her sincere affection for Britain influenced her career in teaching English as a foreign language.

As a university lecturer and Business English teacher she remains an avid observer not only of British society but also of the political landscape in Great Britain.

She lives with her family in the South of Germany.

To my children, Marc, Lisa and Piers who prove to me over and over that children are a blessing.

M. J. Boyle

Empire Close

Austin Macauley Publishers

London • Cambridge • New York • Sharjah

Copyright © M. J. Boyle 2024

The right of M. J. Boyle to be identified as author of this work has been asserted by the author in accordance with sections 77 and 78 of the Copyright, Designs and Patents Act 1988.

All rights reserved. No part of this publication may be reproduced, stored in a retrieval system, or transmitted in any form or by any means, electronic, mechanical, photocopying, recording, or otherwise, without the prior permission of the publishers.

Any person who commits any unauthorised act in relation to this publication may be liable to criminal prosecution and civil claims for damages.

This is a work of fiction. Names, characters, businesses, places, events, locales, and incidents are either the products of the author's imagination or used in a fictitious manner. Any resemblance to actual persons, living or dead, or actual events is purely coincidental.

A CIP catalogue record for this title is available from the British Library.

ISBN 9781035839308 (Paperback)
ISBN 9781035839315 (ePub e-book)

www.austinmacauley.com

First Published 2024
Austin Macauley Publishers Ltd®
1 Canada Square
Canary Wharf
London
E14 5AA

I wish to thank all those who helped me with this project, and without whom this would not have been possible.

First and foremost, Kurt as he is the one who urges me on when I feel drained of ideas and he is the one who gives me the strength to continue.

The continuing interest of my daughter, Lisa, to my projects is a commitment not to be underestimated. I will never take it for granted.

There were so many involved in this project; some gave invaluable information to ensure I stayed on track, some checked and double-checked even the smallest of issues, some gave constructive feedback. You may all rest assured of my sincerest thanks.

Lastly, my thanks to the teams at Austin Macauley for accompanying and supporting me along the road to the publication of *Empire Close*.

Table of Contents

1: Looking Back	12
2: The Gemmells, 6 Empire Close	19
3: The Hutchinsons, 5 Empire Close	30
4: The Fairweathers, 4 Empire Close	34
5: The Selby-Holmes, 3 Empire Close	41
6: The o'Donegals, 2 Empire Close	46
7: The World Turned Upside Down	53
8: The World Keeps Turning	63
9: Number One, Empire Close	71
10: The Depths of Our Loved Ones	78
11: Decisive Moves	83
12: A Change in Perception	88
13: The Wake	95
14: The House of Content	105

A country is not what it does, it is what it tolerates.
— Tucholsky

1
Looking Back

Ted was sitting in his chair in the front room. Of course he was – he couldn't leave it without help and with his carer having already left for the day and his wife not yet home, he was stuck. MS was a bummer, every so often things would get worse, then slightly better, then worse again. He had to come to terms with the fact that he was now confined to the wheelchair. He would never again walk freely and without aid. So, at this moment, he was stuck where he was. But then, maybe "stuck" wasn't quite the right word. From this vantage point he had the most comprehensive view of the close in which he lived, had lived, for almost all of his married life, and that was now 45 years.

So, he sat and saw the picture unravelling. Number 2 had gone up for sale when Michael died. None of his four children had wanted to move in there and, this was his guess, all of them wanted to have the money in the bank. They had made a quick sale and he had been told they had achieved a good price, and now he knew why they had been so cagey about whom they had sold the house to. Not that he could have done anything about it, he was just the neighbour from across the road. It had seemed very peculiar that the children had only collected things in removal boxes, albeit a great number – but then Michael and Mary had been there for a long time and things do pile up. But to leave all the furniture there, was certainly unusual, to say the least. Now it was clear why.

He began to reminisce, revelling in the times gone by and pondering the set-up in the Close.

As a young married couple, he and Meg had moved in to Number One. They had been so proud of their home, still were. It was a four-bedroomed detached house in a cosy cul-du-sac on the Liberty Estate, a development of 80 properties designed to attract young families arriving in the quickly expanding west side of this commuter town he had grown up in.

He had to smile when he recalled the discussions about how the streets should be called. The choice had fallen to past heroes – Nelson Road, Drake Lane, Raleigh Crescent, Wellington Way and Cook Avenue, which proved, in retrospect, wise. Initially, they were to have names of countries in the British Empire and all, but all, of the countries chosen – Cyprus, Malaya, Singapore, Uganda and Barbados – were no longer part of the Empire less than twenty years later. Our street, though, thought Ted, our street had its name right from the start: "Empire Close". Meg's parents had given them the deposit. God rest their souls, and his parents had paid the lion's share of the interior costs; the wallpapering, the wall-to-wall carpets, the built-in bedroom cupboards, and the kitchen units. He would like to think they had never regretted it, but when he thought of the seemingly never-ending comments from his father when they ripped up the carpets and had wooden floors laid, he wasn't too sure.

His mother almost went crazy when they mentioned replacing the kitchen units, but then that was a flash in the pan and she unfortunately didn't live long enough to see how grand it all looked after the make-over – almost 15 years later.

My, thought Ted, what a privileged life we have actually had. How many newlyweds could be given such a send-off in those days? We did appreciate it, even if we never really said so. It was difficult expressing emotions like that in those days. Ted did wonder, had that really changed? Whatever. We showed it in that we looked after all of them – right up to the end. Right up to the end and in spite of all the difficulties it had occasionally caused. The leukaemia which took Meg's mother so fast was, looking back, a blessing when one compared it with the long and drawn out agony of the stomach cancer which put an end to Meg's father's life.

Ted's mum died in the hospital after an operation – it was a routine operation the doctor had said beforehand, nothing to worry about. So, no one had worried. Then everyone was devastated. She simply didn't wake up again after the operation. Ted's father was diagnosed with Alzheimer's, this proved to be a test-and-a-half for poor Meg. She had to deal with him day in, day out, it wasn't easy for her. It was her idea to convert the study into a bedroom for him and to add a shower area into the downstairs wet unit. She was there for him and helped him, suffered immensely under his, albeit verbal, attacks. He had been so hurtful in what he had said sometimes. She bore it all like a saint. That was her way of saying "Thank you". Ted was sure of that. Ted was grateful to their parents, too. But he also knew that without his own endeavours and his damned hard work, their lives would not have been so cosy, either.

They had a right to be proud of their achievements in their own right. Yes, maybe they had been given a good head-start, but they had been tested with ups and downs and they had prevailed. They had the spirit of good citizens in them, good British citizens. Just like all the others in the Close. Every single one of them.

And now Michael was no more. They hadn't really liked each other at first. But Ted knew in his heart of hearts that it was his fault. He hadn't given Michael a fair go at getting close. There had been prejudices holding him back. So silly in retrospect, but at the time they were all-embracing. Michael and his wife were both Irish. 'So what?' one could say now, but then it was a completely different kettle of fish. Ted felt a pang of remorse when he tallied the amount of time, friendship time, that they, no he, had let slide in those early years. It had been almost half a decade before they actually really got on proper neighbourhood terms. Half a decade in which both families had grown, thus developing into almost like-minded units. Both units wanting only the best for their children.

If only I could put the clock back, mused Ted. Admittedly, sometimes he had thought Michael was riding for a fall. He would bet on anything that moved, and he would down the pints like they were going out of fashion. But he had a heart of gold, if you needed a hand you just had to say the word and he would be there. He had played a good innings, even if he only reached the autumn of his life, indeed he was only two years older! Oh, I could go on for ever thinking about that family, thought Ted, we have so many memories – and now he's gone.

But then, not only he was gone. Everyone else was gone, as well. All of them. None left – except him and Meg. A respected community in a respectable Close.

It had been the early 1950s and things were looking up. Life was becoming more and more comfortable as time went on. National service was still around as a constant reminder of the war, but most of the rationing was over and folks could settle down to a peaceful life.

One aspect which Ted had thought at the time rather put the cat among the pigeons was the Nationality Act of 1948 giving all imperial subjects the right to free entry into post-war Britain. He had considered this to be a step too far, but he had kept his powder dry and his mouth shut. When London Transport went and paid for thousands of new employees to come in from Barbados, he had thought that was enough to make the angels weep, but he kept his thoughts to himself and his life in order. He had done his duty, served his country, been there when it needed him and now just wanted to reap the benefit of being on the winning side. In Ted's mind, one benefit should be that Britons could now get on with their lives, in peace, and in ever-increasing comfort. Britons being persons born in Britain and of British heritance. British for Ted, was a question of breeding, of blood and his British education had instilled in him a patriotic nuance coupled with a strong feeling of national pride. It was for this reason that Ted was extremely glad to have been able to procure his marital home in a Close such as Empire Close.

Yes, it was a privilege to live here.

What fun we had in those days! In those post-war days, when community awareness and a sense of patriotism and pride – yes, I will separate them, thought Ted – were so predominant. We were all pulling together to make the best future, for ourselves, for our families and for our country. At the drop of a hat, someone would organise a street party. Due to the fact that the Close was a dead-end, no one but them would want to enter it. They had a free hand in what they did. Just decide there was to be a party, and Bob's your uncle. If it rained, or if the party was a birthday celebration in a colder month, they simply staged it in Number 4's garage. They were the only ones with a large garage. Quite something in those days. Every year they had the biggest do on 24th May – Empire Day. Flags galore hanging from every house and everyone would recite something, or sing an Empire song they had learnt at school: *What can I do for England that does so much for me …* was a favourite. Every one of them wanted to feel part of the glorious Empire, although it was, admittedly, falling apart around them. We had to stop celebrating around 1957, or was it 1958. Can't remember exactly, thought Ted.

He tried hard, but it was no good: Never mind, whenever it was, it somehow wasn't quite the same after that, what with the changing face of the Close and the changing name of celebration – Commonwealth Day. Didn't have quite the same ring to it as Empire Day. Everyone had joined in with the fun, no one felt aloof. We would all muddle-in and each family would bring food and drink. Someone – who was it? Ted couldn't remember that either – had a record player which they brought along and we'd play old records. The younger ones had different records to us, obviously. Their music was different, too. My goodness, remembered Ted, what we didn't think about the Beatles when they first came out with that so-called "pop" music. We even had some Rolling Stones records, not that anyone danced to that, though. We were all too busy contemplating the lyrics. They were right rebels, those Rolling Stones He felt it important, to note that the

Close itself was not a rebel community. We were all true Brits and were proud of it. The strains of the war could be forgotten and the new age was well on its way to offering a good life for all. Food, drink, music, and dancing – with not a care in the world.

Oh yes, we were such a good lot. Always time for a chat and always time for a party. That was Empire Close. There were only six houses in all in the Close. A "close" community, quite literally. All filled with couples striving to make their mark and attain the life and the success to which they thought they were entitled.

Looking back, thought Ted, maybe Number 6 had been a slight disappointment.

2
The Gemmells, 6 Empire Close

There was one event – or maybe trail of events – which Ted did have to admit had tainted the reputation of the Close. Why, it had even left the house at the end of the Close, empty for quite a while. First, due to the circumstances, and then due to the fact that no buyer could be found.

At the tail-end were the houses – Number 5 (on the left-hand side) and Number 6 (on the right-hand side) The couple in Number 6 had a bumpy marriage. The husband seemed on the square. A man of few words, and the wife played fast and loose, not that she flaunted herself in the Close, but she did have a reputation. Muriel Gemmell was a stunner and she knew it. She was a favourite with the men at the British Legion Club and no one was really surprised when she left poor old Desmond down in the dumps. Seems she found a better catch on her rounds and she went to live with him in his house in Scotland. At least that was what Meg had told him. Fact was, she disappeared from the Close from one day to the next. Ted had quite missed her, not that he had allowed himself any thoughts about her beyond those of a curious neighbour, simply watching the way she paraded down the street when she went out for the evening – or even when she was just going shopping. She was an eyeful. Ted had often thought she could have entered a beauty competition and would have won hands down. He had no idea of her personality; Meg had always been very wary of getting into too close a relationship with her and Desmond. Ted had to smile at this – yes, Meg was actually jealous! And, as for Desmond, well, Desmond was a weird chap. Rumour had it that he worked for an insurance company. He had never really said which insurance company, or what he did there. He was, in fact, quite a mystery. One thing was for sure, he wasn't a rep. He never, in all his time in the Close, called on any of the other residents and tried to sell them an insurance policy.

There were rumours, so Meg had informed him, that he may have been a spy. Just imagine that, a real live Le Carré spy living in such proximity. Fact was, he was often away for days on end, "on business" was the official narrative. No one bothered to ask, no one wanted to be assessed as being too nosy. Maybe it was fear which kept us all quiet? pondered Ted. No, that wasn't it – in those days everyone kept themselves to themselves when it came to personal matters. Minding their own business and going their own way. Ted had later remembered that Paul (from number 5) had spoken of rather loud arguments in the Gemmell household, followed by rather loud music being played – everyone assumed that was accompaniment for the peace-making process. Ted couldn't help but smile, we all had quite a laugh about that, joking that the peace-making exercise should have been a love-making exercise and then maybe they would have stayed together. She was to be a resident of the close for a mere two years and by 1954, she was gone.

Desmond mooched around, avoiding eye-contact and any kind of conversation with anyone at all for what seemed like a lifetime. He still went away on his "business trips", then returned, mooched a little more and headed off again.

The Close community were beginning to get a little worried about the house – what with no one there to care for it – then all of a sudden, Desmond acquired a new lease of life. One day he showed up with a new wife. He had been alone for around two years when love struck him like a flash of lightening and he (almost instantly it seemed) married a woman from Wales, who he had met at work. At least, that was what he had said. Everyone was so pleased that something akin to order was back that no real questions were asked.

Monica was such a pleasant woman, had a smile for everyone she met and always time for a chat. She could talk nineteen to the dozen that woman. Admittedly, she was a little mum when it came to talking about Desmond's job, but other than that, if you wanted some info from town, she was the one to ask. Never stopped smiling, never stopped chatting and never got pregnant.

She seemed content enough with her lot, in fact we were all sorry to see her go. 1960 it must have been. Word had it – no one really knew for sure – that they moved to Wales so that Monica could be near her parents.

The house went on the market and literally within days the "for sale" sign was removed.

None of us thought anything about it at the time, recalled Ted as he readjusted his sitting position. Where on earth was Meg? She couldn´t possibly need so much time just to buy some potatoes and some ham. That woman would try the patience of a saint. I'll have to have words with her when she gets back, she just isn't taking this new phase of my MS seriously. I can't be left on my own anymore.

His thoughts returned to Number 6. He remembered only too well the shock when the new owners turned up. It was a Saturday afternoon, sun shining and everyone (except the Fairweathers from Number 4 who were, as always, in town on some official business) was out front, washing the cars. The newcomers got out of the car and you could almost feel the air tense up.

The driver had a turban on, that in itself was not a problem, for he could well be the chauffeur, such was the car. But then the rest of the family got out. They obviously belonged together, were obviously a family. The driver went to the front door and opened it with his key. So now we all knew – these were the new neighbours.

I suppose it must have looked really peculiar, reflected Ted, we probably all turned around and started rubbing the car like crazy – merely to ensure that there was no eye-contact. This was something which needed to be digested before any comment, or indeed contact, was made.

It was actually more glances than comments that were exchanged. The Selby-Holmes were furious, they had perceived this as the kiss of death to the prestigious Close, they had told Meg that in no uncertain terms over the garden fence.

The Fairweathers were much more reserved in their outward remarks. As prominent personalities of the town, they obviously felt a need to test the waters first. It was, however, to hail a period of rather minimised (both in numbers of participants and in fun-factor) street parties in the Close. The Fairweathers were simply not interested and steered clear of them. Michael was a different kettle of fish, of course he was. Always ready to nail his colours to the mast, he proclaimed they were "a nasty piece of work" and we should be wary of accepting them into the fold. Funny that, contemplated Ted, that it should have been Michael and Mary, the only non-Brits in the Close, who should be so against the newcomers. It didn't stop Michael being Michael though, he was happy to play the waiting game – he was certain they wouldn't be around for long. How right he turned out to be. They were Sikhs, in fact. To be fair, they were actually respectable citizens. Ted could not remember a single occasion when they were not friendly, attentive and yes, caring. There was that time when Meg fell on the pavement and sprained her ankle. It was the woman from Number 6 who helped her up, the son who carried her indoors and set her down on the couch. They made her a cup of tea and called the doctor, recalled Ted. They didn't leave her side until Ted had arrived home to be with her. My God, thought Ted, with a certain pang of embarrassment, he couldn't even remember their names. Seems they always were, and always would be simply the neighbours from Number 6. They really did keep to themselves in ways that made everyone else perceive them as aloof. They never really joined in any of the parties – but, even when they did, they came for the start, just to prove they had received the note, but always left when the BBQ started or when the drink really started flowing. They never touched any alcohol and never touched any meat. It then dawned on Ted: we had a street party once on Grand National day and Michael wanted everyone to pitch in and we'd have an "Empire Close" bet – he had a really good tip as to which horse was going to win. Not Number 6, though – they weren't having any of it. Gambling was another of their no-goes. Wise choice as it fanned out – Michael's horse fell at the third fence.

There were all sorts of nasty rumours flying around about Sikhs at the time but Ted couldn't contend to them when it came to Number 6. They always seemed clean and well-groomed – OK, who knows what their hair was like under the turbans – the lad had told Meg we should call them Dastars. He was so proud when he got his after turning twelve. Paraded it, walking up and down the street for everyone to see. Until then his hair had been long, but neatly kept, never looked filthy. But then, thought Ted, what would I know, I hardly ever saw them. I tried to keep out of their way. I didn't know what to say to them. I suppose it was the fear of the unknown, or maybe that I was afraid I might say something I would regret later. I was quite unfair to them.

Isn't it funny, thought Ted, how time can heal such feelings? Back then, I was quite angry that they had arrived in our Close. Naturally, I merely listened to Francis when he got going on the subject, but I actually shared the view of the Selby-Holmes' next door that they were bringing the price of our property down, merely with their presence in the Close. Even more so when the extended family appeared and it seemed there were about eight of them all living together in the house. I mean, it only had three bedrooms. Where on earth did they all sleep?

The Fairweathers at Number 4 did all they could, pulled all the favours possible to block permission to build that pavilion thing in the garden. They didn't have a leg to stand on really, there was no way they could even see it from their house. It was to go up in the back garden and was to be no higher than the hedge – which had by then reached quite a height. But then, Ted reminded himself, the Fairweathers always did think there were special rules for them and that if they were against something, well, it could simply be swept away. No such luck, some chap from the council came (obviously his brown envelope had not been padded enough), checked everything out, and permission was granted, albeit with the specification that a proper foundation must be laid.

Whether this was to be "luck" or not, was to be seen just weeks later when the digger arrived to start the foundation work. Ted arrived home to find the Close full of police cars. They didn't even want to let him into the Close, at all. All cordoned off. Press, and photographers all over the place. Ted had been quite perplexed at the whole thing as he wandered across the road to check on Michael – maybe he knew what was going on.

As he strode across, he saw two men being taken out of Number 6 and escorted to – separate – police cars and driven away. There we have it, he had thought, I knew all along, no good would come of this.

Michael, of course did know what was what. It seems the digger had uncovered a secret. A corpse buried in the back garden. Well, they should have buried it a little deeper, shouldn't they? Michael had said, law of the jungle and all that. The two men had laughed at the stupidity of the folks at Number 6.

Michael and Ted had sat together in the front room and drunk beer after beer, watching and speculating. They had been sure this was the turning point. This would be the end of the Sikh household in Empire Close.

Of course, the two of them had always known that something was amiss with that lot. Why, they had probably been keeping themselves to themselves for this very reason – so no one would know who actually lived there and who had gone missing. You really can't be too careful these days, they had decided.

In the days to follow, Ted and Meg were questioned numerous times by the police. It had seemed funny. At first they were questioned about the family – the comings and goings at Number 6. If they had noticed anything unusual, peculiar. Well, no. They were Sikhs and they kept themselves to themselves. Then suddenly the questioning changed completely.

The police were more interested in the Gemmells. Wanted to know all sorts of things. This was, naturally easier to answer. Meg knew a lot about Monica, they had often chatted, although Meg did then say that it was difficult to get a word in edgeways once Monica got started on something. And Ted knew a lot about Desmond – or at least he thought he did until he started answering the questions. He realised that all he knew was that Desmond worked for an insurance company, went on business trips often, drank a lot, was divorced, adored his second wife and had suffered under his first wife's affairs.

The police eventually found Desmond living in Devon with a third wife. Poor Monica had apparently died in a car accident not long after they had moved away.

The police went looking for Muriel in Scotland. She was not to be found – not in Scotland. She had, in fact, never left Empire Close.

Shockwaves hit Empire Close. It was not the Sikh household; it was Desmond Gemmell to blame for all the unfortunate publicity.

How easy it had been to believe that the foreigners were the guilty ones. Come to think of it, thought Ted, how easy it had been to consider the Sikhs as foreigners.

Desmond was found guilty of murdering Muriel. He had apparently strangled her to death. He was sentenced to life imprisonment. Capital punishment had not yet been abolished, that came almost seven years later, but for some reason the judge saw fit to impose life imprisonment on the "unfortunate" chap. Did Desmond have some leverage in court, after all? thought Ted, and whilst on the subject of Desmond – was Monica's accident really an accident?

How can one misread a person to such an extent? Why, we lived in such close proximity for 8 years in all. Even Meg hadn't noticed, but then she had steered clear of Muriel, hadn't she?

Where the hell is she, thought Ted, not like Meg to be gone for such a long time.

Whatever, Empire Close had had its five minutes of fame – the street was in all town conversations and subject of every pub chat for many months. Even hit the national headlines for a while. Crime tourists were a common sight every weekend, everyone wanted to see the house and the garden where the corpse had been found. The rest of us just had to bear it.

It all proved too much for the Sikh household. They left lock, stock and barrel within the year and put the house up for sale. There was a lot of interest but, as Meg had said, it was just curiosity. The people coming to look were fooling the estate agents, they weren't buyers at all. They just wanted to see where it all had happened. Soak up some of the horror and the mystery and dwell in some apparent mystery. Who in their right mind would want to live there after such a crime?

The damage was done.

It was almost eight months before the "for sale" sign disappeared for good. The Nowaks bought the house.

The Nowaks were, no are, basically a pleasant enough family. Poles, I think. Somehow, noted Ted, we just never really wanted to get to know them. Desmond had somehow ruined the setting. The woman's name is Magda, I think, thought Ted, yes, that's what Meg said. Magda, unfortunate name really, but she was quite a fashion queen. Mary Quant style clothing, that was what Meg called it – for Ted it had seemed slightly daring, whatever it was called. But, nice to look at, all the same.

Ted's thoughts which were concentrating themselves around Magda's long legs, were interrupted by the ring of the telephone. Ted couldn't answer it. There was no way he could get to the hallway before the answering machine kicked in. So, he just listened closely to get the message – should one be left. So many people just don't bother to leave messages. It was his son, Ian. As a businessman he was used to this new technology and he did leave a message. He was in Belgium on a business trip until the following Wednesday. He'd call again when he returned.

Ted often wondered if it were a curse or a blessing that he was now in retirement. Nowadays global business was commonplace and everyone seemed to be travelling around the world to do their deals. Was this a good thing?

As a chartered accountant Ted had spent his working life in an office in the city. He had commuted every morning in and every evening home. He had been able to do all his business from his office. If someone needed his services, they had come to him. Meetings were always face-to-face and you always knew the people you were working for and with. Ted had been to conferences, of course he had, but they were always in England somewhere and only ever two days long – meaning only one night away from home. In truth, Ted felt quite sorry for modern day working folk, it must be very tiring and a terrific strain on any relationship, be it marital or "wild".

3
The Hutchinsons, 5 Empire Close

Ted adjusted the blanket which was spread across his legs. There was a nip in the air. When Meg gets back, she'll have to turn the heating up a little, somehow sitting around doing nothing was not a good way of keeping warm. Memories though, reflected Ted, memories keep me warm. I have such good memories of our life here. He felt truly sorry for people who lost their memory in old age. Mind you, he thought, what is old age? I'm not even 75 yet there's plenty of life in this dog still. So where does "old" start?

He snuggled down a little into the chair and returned to the past. Funny how it had been the two houses at the end that had let us all down, he said to himself. Number 6 was definitely a hard one to match, but Number 5 to the left of it, certainly turned out to be a slap in the face for such model citizens as the rest of us in the Close. Everything had started out so well.

I remember only too well, conceived Ted that we all had to watch our spending. Make do with what you have and repair what goes bust, that was everyone's motto. We were all in the same boat that made it easier. The whole country had been ruined by the war and was nigh-on bankrupt and the people were exhausted, some even broken by what they had experienced. No one really wanted to talk about it – just try and forget the worst bits and set one's sights on the future.

Number 5 had still been empty when Ted and Meg first moved in. The house was completely finished and had been sold but the owners had yet to move in. Ted had never asked why they had moved in so much later than expected, he didn't want to appear too nosy, after all Meg was the one who asked the questions in their house.

Ted and Meg had enough to do anyway, getting their own house sorted. Their first house, little did they know then that it would remain their home for such a long time. If I recall correctly, it must have been a good four months before Paul and Hilda Hutchinson arrived with their three-year-old daughter, Nora, thought Ted. Hilda was obviously pregnant; the bump was in full bloom. Meg had looked on with envy, she could hardly wait to be pregnant herself. All the more distraught was she when, only a few weeks later, poor Hilda fell down the stairs and lost the baby.

Paul's parents were local landowners and they farmed the complete area to the west of the town. Paul, as second son, was not in line for the farm, nor did he seem to be particularly interested in it. He was quite happy to leave that kind of work to his elder brother, Will. He was quite happy to be "bailed out" as he so often called it, felt he had done his bit anyway, by enlisting, much to his Father's disgust. It was thus his parents´ money that had secured the family the house in Empire Close. Paul was a teacher in his first post at the local secondary modern school. He taught Geography and he was very sporty in his free time, always running around in his track suit and always trying to get everyone else in the Close to go running with him – he never managed it. He was the life and soul of every get-together and everyone, but everyone, liked him. His colleagues, his pupils, the parents and the neighbours. He had a smile and jolly chat waiting for you whenever you met up with him. He took part in the local marathon race, must have been 1955 – he was 54th – everyone celebrated together with a party in the road. Everyone brought something along, it was such a laugh. Life was so care-free, then. So much so, that no one noticed the change in Hilda.

After losing the baby Hilda withdrew from the community, that is how they saw it. Meg tried hard to keep contact with her but she didn't know how to reach her.

Sometimes she wouldn't even open the front door. She simply ignored the knocking, however long Meg waited. When they did see her walking to the shops or in the garden, or just through the front window, she always looked sullen. Meg noticed that she lost a lot of weight and that her hair hung down framing her face and was as forlorn and dull as her manner. Sometimes they wouldn't see her for days on end, she didn't even go shopping – poor Paul had to do it all himself. It had seemed that the more extroverted Paul became, the more introverted Hilda became. Little Nora always put on a brave face, she was such a lovely little girl. They took her away in the end.

Paul's parents came one day and packed up all Nora's belongings and put them in the car. They placed Nora in the back seat and drove her away. To this very day Ted could remember the way that brave girl waved to the neighbours as she was driven away to her grandparent's home. Hilda left without saying a word to anyone – not even to Meg. Paul continued smiling and pretending all was well while packing up all the belongings in the house and he finally left the Close behind after only four years of residence. Town-talk spoke of him moving to a flat, town-talk also spoke of the fact that he had regularly beaten his wife. Whatever he had done, it had severely blotted his copybook. From what Meg had heard, the truth had come out when he started beating Hilda in front of Nora who then confided in her grandmother. That was the last straw, that was when they came and took Nora with them. Ted had often wondered why they had taken Nora but left Hilda to fend for herself. As far as Ted was concerned, if these stories were all true, and he did have his doubts as Paul was such a good chap, then surely the old Hutchinsons would have helped Hilda in some way. Nought so strange as folks, concluded Ted.

It was the Wang family that then bought the house and have been there ever since. They were Chinese and hardly spoke any English. Always smiled and bowed when they saw anyone, regardless of whether they knew them or not. I suppose that must be a culture thing, thought Ted. They were entrepreneurs then, retired entrepreneurs now, although I do see them going off every morning and only coming home at night. Maybe that's a culture thing as well, they just can't stop. Don't know when to hand over the reins. They owned (probably still own) the Laundry in town. The extended family have set up quite an imperium now, or so Meg says. They have the Chinese restaurant in town and, if town-talk can be believed, a chain of more than ten others, and that is alongside the multiple Chinese Take-Aways under their control. Ted speculated: they won't be returning home to China any time soon, I guess.

4
The Fairweathers, 4 Empire Close

Ted heard the key turning in the front door – at long last Meg was back from shopping.

'Hi, Love. I'm back!' Meg shouted from the hallway as she hung up her coat and took off her shoes. She picked up the shopping basket and walked past the living room into the kitchen at the back of the house. She heard Ted shout, 'What the hell took you so long?' She paused, this really was getting impossible. She couldn't do a damn thing anymore without him commenting on the fact that she spent too much time out of the house. She put the kettle on and wandered through the dining area to the front room where Ted was sitting gazing out into the Close. He looked up when she came in, 'I was getting worried.' 'I was only out for an hour.' 'No, it was much longer than that.' 'Where's Dolly?' 'I told her she could go home, that you'd be back in no time. You only wanted to get potatoes and some ham. I didn't think that would take that long.' 'I met Jeannie and she just had to give me the latest news on Mrs Fairweather, well, ex-Mrs Fairweather.' 'Silly woman, she was.' 'Well, she stuck up for her husband and he had no better gratitude to offer than cheating on her. Mind you, she should have known which side of the bread was buttered.' 'So, what's the big news now, then?'

'I'll get us some tea and tell. Hold on a tick.'

The Fairweathers had lived at Number 4. Although they had left the Close in 1972 – so, a good 25 years ago – news about them was always of interest as Geoffrey had been a beacon of society in the town. He was – or rather had been – the local MP. This had made him a popular target for the local press and, although it was mostly favourable, they did have a harder dig every now and again. Probably it was felt that this had to be in order to keep up with the big shots in Fleet Street, that was the new normal, for politicians were definitely subjected to more scrutiny in the 70s than ever before. He was remembered by all as very popular and very outspoken. Although he was not one to tell tales out of school, he did have a mine of information on which to fall back on and could always say just enough to make you feel he was telling you something that was not common knowledge and always managed to have you reading between the lines. Ted had never been completely sure just how honest he was with everyone, but then, he did seem to have the interest of his constituents at heart when he trotted off down to Westminster. My goodness, thought Ted, he must be going on for 90 by now. Victoria, his wife, was slightly younger than him; she was a lovely woman, always had a smile on her face and always well-dressed, whatever the time of day and wherever she was going. They had two children, a boy and a girl. Both went to university and then were hardly ever seen again. They must be in their sixties by now as well, how time flies past. My goodness, thought Ted, that was some stir old Geoffrey caused when he came out in support of, what was his name? Martin, Martin Lindsay. Yes, that was it – the Conservative MP for Solihull. Even though he had never been one to mince his words, a lot of folk were surprised by that. Multiracial society was endangering the national character, or something like that, it was. Geoffrey took a while to get over that but by the 70s it had all blown over, at least for Geoffrey.

Meg arrived with a tray laden with two mugs of tea and a plate of shortbread biscuits.

'Did Dolly have anything to say for herself today?' asked Meg, genuinely interested. 'No, not really. She did mention her son had a cold, her daughter had had a nasty bout of asthma and was home from school, oh, and that her husband had been laid off,' answered Ted, genuinely uninterested. 'So, that is more a YES then, I would say. Good heavens, Ted, have you no sympathy? You didn't use to be like this – the Ted I knew was the most empathic man around. And now listen to you – so hard-hearted.' 'It's this bloody wheelchair – bogging me down – making me cynical and bad-tempered. Why me? That's what I want to know? Why me?' 'At least you're better off than Victoria Fairweather.' 'Why? What's she got, then?' 'She's dead.' Meg took a sip of her tea. 'And you say I′m hard-hearted!' Ted took a sip of his tea, 'What did she die of?' 'According to Jeannie, she had a heart attack and didn't get attention in time.' 'Was she living on her own?' 'Yes. And no panic button to come to the rescue. Seems her cleaning lady found her the next morning. It was much too late to do anything by then. Do you think we should go to the funeral?' 'We were neighbours for 20 years, I suppose we should really.' 'Those were the days, weren't they?' 'Oh yes, indeed. I was perusing some of those memories while you were out. Do you remember the "farewell" party we had in the Fairweather's garage when the Beatles announced they were splitting up? Not to mention the uproar the corpse in

Number 6's garden caused? Geoffrey almost took it personally.' 'Oh don't remind me! Mind you it wasn't half as bad as the shock when the Sikhs first moved in, was it?' 'Will Geoffrey be at the funeral, do you think?'

'I should think so they were married for almost 40 years. Why did she do that do you think?' 'What, divorce him, you mean? I guess to pay him back. She probably felt he wasn't being grateful enough for what she had done for him.' 'It certainly saved his skin – at least for a while.' 'Just goes to show, you have to be careful who you trust.' 'You should be able to trust your wife – I certainly wouldn't turn on you like that.' 'I wouldn't knock someone down and drive away though, would I?' 'OK. True. It must have been the shock of the moment that made him do it. He was such a nice man.' 'Yes, he was. I think he may have been drunk. Those headlines would not have looked good, would they? He couldn't possibly stay and face the music.'

'At least they did admit it was their car that was in the accident. They didn't try to hide that. That must have cost quite a lot of courage to step forward in that way. Victoria always was a strong person.' 'Don't be daft. They had to admit it. The woman gave the police the car registration number. Anyway, if she were that strong, she would have kept quiet. She wouldn't have put the dagger in his back after the affair with his secretary, would she?' 'I suppose he hurt her feelings and she was feeling spiteful, then once it is out, it's out and there's no turning back, is there?' 'No. What else could he do once she'd confessed to lying about the accident?' 'Perverting the course of justice! She got her dues.' 'And he was left sweeping up the mess. Is he still with that secretary? Do you know?' 'No. That was over before the divorce was even declared, or so I heard.' 'I wonder how the children dealt with all that publicity.' 'I guess, we'll never know. You know what, I think we should go to the funeral – maybe we can have a chat with Geoffrey – for old time's sake.'

'Yes, would be good. I would like to know what he feels about politics today. He was such a strong fighter for us all. Do you think he feels they are doing such a good job today? Would definitely be interesting to find out.' 'It'll be in the newspaper – the date of the funeral,' said Meg as she left the living room heading for the kitchen. It was time to start getting the dinner ready.

By the time dinner was on the table Meg had got herself into quite a tizzy. 'I'm guessing those tears in your eyes aren't from the onions,' said Ted, making an, admittedly feeble, attempt to liven things up a bit. 'No. Sorry. Know I should be well over it by now but us talking about the past earlier just made me remember 1962, the year Mum died. I just can't help myself. It was so sudden and so unjust.' 'Stop it, Meg. Don't do this to yourself. It was leukaemia – no one could do anything about it.' 'She was only 59. Hardly time to get to know Ian and never sharing our pride in Rosemary's riding successes.'

'Tragic as it was, it was quick. We have to be thankful for small mercies. Not like me here. I'm burdened with this for the rest of my life, which may well be quite a while.' 'Doctor Williams says you'll not be dancing a jig ever again but you can still have quality of life which many people would give their bottom drawers for.' Ted couldn't help but smile at this – he'd never danced a jig in his life. 'Let's have some wine with the dinner, Meg. We really do have so much we should be grateful for – let '62 lie.' Meg went to the wine rack in the corner and found a bottle of Californian Red. 'This should do the trick – you open it and I'll get the glasses.'

Once poured, they drank a sip. 'Well, there you go,' said Ted, 'it pays to have a low room temperature. This is perfect.'

'Were you cold this afternoon, then?' 'Yes, I had wanted to get you to turn the heating up when you got home, but somehow it slipped my mind.' 'Any talk of politics and you can get heated up,' laughed Meg. 'Did you actually miss them when they moved out? The Fairweathers, I mean.' 'In a way, yes, I did. They gave the Close a real sense of prestige, don't you think? We were part of their world, weren't we? They talked to us as neighbours, we were one of them.' 'And then off they went and we never saw, or heard from them again. Not even a Christmas card.' 'Guess they had more enhancing things to deal with.' 'Like life, you mean?' 'And Parliament back-office.'

'Do you remember when the Almonds moved into the house?' 'Oh yes, just before Christmas it was. You sent them a Christmas card and they sent it back because you had spelt their name wrong.' 'How was I to know that it was a Jewish name? Who could have imagined spelling it like that A-L-M-O-N. How fussy can you get? They're still fussy about it today, I bet.' 'Didn't stop you baby-sitting for them, did it?' 'Don't start that again, Ted. Leave it be, please!'

'I'm just saying, just because they introduced that Race Relations Act didn't mean we all had to jump up and down and sing hallelujah when persons of other religions appeared on your doorstep – or in this case, in your Close.'

'Be fair, Ted. That Act was necessary. Things were getting out of hand. Just because someone is of a different culture, or has a different skin colour you can't stop them buying houses, or getting jobs or receiving help, can you?'

5
The Selby-Holmes, 3 Empire Close

Ted had a slight headache when he woke up the next morning. He was convinced it had something to do with the way he had been lying in bed. He convinced himself it had nothing to do with the fact that he was slightly unnerved by Meg's political views. She had never spoken to him like that before, well, never about politics. He didn't think she was interested. Meg acknowledged his headache, gave him a fizzy drink (without mentioning the fact that it was hangover treatment), and brushed aside any pity. She was convinced it had more to do with the fact that he had allowed himself two glasses of whiskey after the meal than the way he laid in bed. They didn't argue about it, each of them knew they were right and so they just left it at that.

As it was Wednesday, Meg had to leave at 10:00. She helped out at the food bank on Mondays, Wednesdays and Fridays and she had promised to be in early today as Mandy had a doctor's appointment and would be in later. This was not to Ted's liking. Ted had assumed that once he retired Meg would be there for him. And now of all the 188,000 charities that there were in England she had to go and choose one that had her out of the house three times a week. He felt his nose had been poked out of joint and made a point of outwardly showing his contempt every time she went there. As a means of opposition, this was not well-founded. Meg was all the more determined to go. Not least because Dr Williamson had explained to her that Ted's condition could very possibly improve if he were left to his own devices every so often.

Ted had decided that he wanted to be seated in the bay window – at least until Dolly came to see about him and his lunch. So, that was where Meg left him – seated in the armchair (he had flatly refused to stay in the wheelchair – my God he could be stubborn) and facing the Close.

He realised shortly after Meg had left that this had not been a good decision. In his wheelchair he could change the angle of his view – in this armchair, he could not. He was forced to look at the front garden of Number 3. He closed his eyes but Number 3 did not disappear.

When Ted and Meg had first arrived in the Close, Christopher and Amanda Selby-Holmes were already well-established there – in their home and in the town. Christopher was already 40. Amanda was two years younger. Both were lawyers in the City. Ted remembered thinking: No children – four bedrooms and no children to fill them. What a waste! They were very friendly and had often initiated a chat over the fence at the back. OK, Ted and Meg had never quite made the grade of being invited to one of their extravagant parties but then Ted was never really sure exactly what went on there.

They certainly knew how to live it up. They did seem to have rather flashy parties with a lot of noise and plenty of empty bottles (wine and champagne) to be disposed of next day. Ted had noticed on more than one occasion that only couples were invited and that there was a lot of coming and going the next day. More often than once, all the guests would reappear on the morning after the party and then leave again a short time later. Ted closed his eyes again, yes, now I remember something else – there was a rumour once that they also staged some illegal gambling parties. Those must have been the "quieter" ones. Ted had to smile, they had been so full of fun. Just goes to show doesn't it. Not everyone has to flash around their wealth. They must have had buckets of money – two full salaries from a top-notch legal firm in the city, must have been ample. One could probably almost class it as a licence to print money but then it was said that they knew their beef. If you ever asked them about something legal, they would quote you chapter and verse, far over the heads of anyone else Ted knew. They earned their fortune and they never flaunted it, never snubbed their neighbours. Always smiled and always had a greeting ready. Such lovely people, they were.

Both were from prominent local families and were well-known to all in town. In fact, many saw in them a perfect casting for the positions of Town Mayor – and his Lady Wife. Somehow that didn't turn out quite as they had planned. Maybe there was something in that rumour about the gambling parties. When they left the Close, Ted couldn't quite recall when but it was not long after the World Cup when England won, so maybe in '67, it was said that they went to live in Spain. Strange that. They never really said where they were moving to and, come to think of it, they never sent us any Christmas cards either, although they knew where we were. We just assumed that they had left rather hurriedly and secretly so that they wouldn't have to explain to us, or anybody else, why they had sold the house to "Big Joe".

Big Joe was infamous. He had money but everyone knew it was not come by legally. The only people who seemingly didn't know anything, were the police. Big Joe was of Italian descent, so very probably his fortune had a slight mafia scent to it. He was called Big Joe because he was huge. A giant of a man, someone you wouldn't wish to meet in a dark alley at night – actually not the kind of man you would wish to meet up with anywhere at any time. Meg was scared of him from the first moment she saw him standing on the doorstep. He had come round to say "hello". He wanted to invite all the neighbours to his idea of a house-warming.

They were going to throw a party – with everyone from the Close welcome. Of course, Meg and Ted had attended. It had been quite a party – the first of many in the Amartis' house. Although it was the first and last that Meg and Ted went to. There was an aura of "the devil looks after his own" inside the house, so Ted and Meg decided it was better to play it safe and watch from a distance. Indeed, Big Joe did keep a very low profile beyond the Close.

Big Joe had been their neighbour for almost 15 years.

Although they had brushed off the Winter of Discontent side-by-side (admittedly neither of them would have wanted to be on the receiving end of 60 pounds a week, although for both a 35-hour week may have seemed inviting), and celebrated Charles and Diana's wedding together in the street, in all that time they had never warmed to either the man, nor his family.

He had never returned from a trip to Italy in 1982, but his family had stayed on. If the police were to ask Ted today what he knew of his neighbours to the left, he would be finished quickly in his tale. For, without lying he could safely say, that he knew nothing other than their family relationship to each other. Big Joe's wife, Caterina; with Matteo and his wife Bianca and their two children. The other son, Enzo lived with his wife, Guilia and their three children somewhere in town. The names of the five grandchildren neither Ted nor Meg knew. Nor were they interested.

By the time Dolly arrived Ted was fast asleep in the armchair – those painkillers certainly made one dozy.

6
The o'Donegals, 2 Empire Close

'I'm going to go to the cemetery tomorrow,' said Meg as they sat in the living room watching television. The news had just finished, it was time to decide whether to watch further, to finish their game of scrabble, or to read. 'I want to go and tell Mary and Michael what their children have done.' 'They'll not be giving you an answer, you know.' 'Don't be like that. I need to get this off my chest. There's no point in talking to the children, is there? Too late for that now. But they should know, even if it has them turning in their graves.' 'I'd come with you if I could.'

The o'Donegals had lived opposite Ted and Meg for all those years. Right from the start; from 1952, right up until just a few months ago. Good old Michael and Mary, his wife. Not hard to detect the Irish descent, neither in the names, nor in the accents. They hadn't tried to hide it, not really. And, recalled Ted, Michael only once complained that they spelled his name wrong, had claimed his name was spelt Mícheál not Michael. But as they hardly corresponded in writing, it made no difference.

Michael was a medical researcher with the pharmaceutical company just a few miles down the road. Mary had stayed at home and taken care of the house and the children. Four children they had, all respectable citizens and all with hearts of gold. Well, truth be told, the two young boys were actually quite a handful for Mary, she certainly had her work cut out with them, they were always up to some kind of mischief and she was constantly having to go to the school having been summoned for a chat with the headmaster. Meg always said poor Mary had had more chats with that headmaster than she'd had hot dinners. But that was all water under the bridge now.

The boys had gathered their experiences and had obviously lost their mischievous streak for now they were both working in banking. One was even at the Bank of England – Michael had only recently said he could give him a talking to now that they had the responsibility for setting the interest rates.

Indeed, both lads had good jobs, by all accounts, and had families of their own. The girls had made good choices, at least that was what Michael never tired of telling his friend, Ted. Clare was married to a university professor and Olive was herself a nurse and was married to a GP somewhere down in Devon. They had indeed done well.

They didn't come home much, which was a constant cause of discomfort for Michael, indeed had been for both him and Mary. They had been so close as a family and now they were strewn across the country and barely saw each other. You would have thought if they were so close, then the children would have come to see their father more often once their mother had died, wouldn't you, mused Ted. But then, they all had lives of their own now and anyway, they knew Michael would not let things get him down. Which he didn't. It was his idea that the two of them learned to play golf. Ted was only too happy to oblige; retirement was not all it was made out to be. Golf was a civilised and healthy hobby, at least it was until this recent stage of MS started to set in. During the last few weeks of Michael's life, they had spent most of their golfing time at the "nineteenth hole". Such was Michael, nothing kept him down, he was a good chap. Mary and Meg had strung up a good rapport with each other right from the word go. They were only two years apart and the children were much the same age so they had plenty to chat about and plenty of tips and tricks to share. Ted knew that Mary was often at the house, he could smell her perfume in the room when he got home from work. He never said anything, of course. He was actually quite pleased that Meg had found a friend she could have tea with and chat. Meg had been devastated when Mary was diagnosed with bowel cancer. It couldn't have hit her harder and she mourned severely when Mary died. It had been almost as bad as when she had lost her parents, Ted had been very worried for a while.

When it came to their respective husbands, though, things panned out decidedly differently. Ted and Michael were two very different types. Ted had seen in Michael a typical Irishman, always a joke on hand and always willing to lift a pint. Not only that, he was a gambler. He would sit down on a Friday afternoon and pick out the horses he would back the next day. He had a subscription of sorts at the local betting shop and often tried to get Ted to come along and enjoy the fun. For Ted however, this was not fun. He would rather stay at home and wash the car, or paint the garage door, or actually anything but go to the betting shop with Michael. He was scared of losing money, for he had absolutely no idea about racing horses. Once he did succumb to Michael's bidding and they went to the greyhound track for a spree. It was, in fact, quite amusing. The atmosphere was incredible – almost contagious. Ted thought Michael must have lost around 50 pounds that day. How on earth was he going to explain that to Mary, he had wondered at the time. In 1967 they had watched Wimbledon "in colour" at Ted's house, Michael had found it humorous beyond limits that Wimbledon, where the main actors all wore white was picked to be the first transmission in colour. What a laugh they all had about that. As time went on, they became very good neighbours, friends even.

They had talked as equals, were there for each other if help was needed and spent at least every other Saturday evening either at one or other of the houses – playing cards, without financial stakes. This was an important aspect as Michael was a snide cheat. Ted sometimes had wondered if Michael could play anything at all without cheating in some way. He had probably already tricked his way through the Pearly Gates. Ted had to smile, Michael was a good sport. He missed him dearly, already, and it was only a brace of shakes since he had been swept up from this world by a massive heart attack.

Ted considered himself a knowledgeable person. He had read the newspaper in the train to work, every morning and evening.

Michael, however, knew so much more – and he had an opinion on just about every topic. Ted had often wondered if Michael had maybe in some way manipulated him in some areas, for Michael had such a winning aura when it came to explaining how situations in the world had developed and he had solutions to most of the world's problems. He reckoned politics as such was a mug's game but he respected those who thought they would give it a go.

My word, thought Ted, what events and disasters we had discussed, analysed and seen off in our time together – the assassination of Lord Mountbatten in 1979, the Chernobyl disaster in 1986, then the Lockerbie disaster in 1988, not to mention the Hillsborough tragedy in 1979 and only last year the Docklands bombing. Suddenly Ted remembered Michael's condemnation of mankind when he heard about the first test tube baby. That must have been around '78. A disaster, he had called it. Saw it as the beginning of the end, an end to sexual reproduction as we know it, he had said. Ted had been slightly taken aback at this outburst. They had actually never spoken about anything to do with sex before. Maybe a comment, or two, about some female's appearance, but not about sex. Not about their intimate relationships with, for example, their wives.

Oh, Michael. I miss you, declared Ted, loudly, in his head, to himself.

Here's hoping you were in heaven half an hour before the devil knew you're dead, thought Ted. This was something Michael often cited when anyone he knew was called to meet the Almighty (another saying Michael would often use)

Well, now he was with his Maker and we are left to tidy up the mess down here – Ted couldn't help but feel just a little angry.

Michael had hardly been cold under the ground when the house was put on the market. Ted and Meg had been quite disappointed that neither of the boys would consider moving in with their family. The estate agent arrived one morning and hammered the sign into the ground and went on a tour of the house with his notepad and pen in his hand. He must have made quite a listing as the sign came back down again not even a week later. Who would be that quick?

Ted and Meg had perused this question many evenings and were puzzled even more when the children arrived one Sunday each carrying boxes and bags as they marched into the house. Just two hours later they were obviously finished with their mission, and left.

Not a word to the neighbours, just imagine that. Peculiar to say the least.

Then the situation became clearer. The house had been sold as a furnished property. The children were leaving their parents furniture in the house! As this became evident, Ted and Meg had an extra whiskey, which they downed as they toasted their old friends, Mary and Michael. Why, if they knew what was going on here, they would both turn in their graves.

It was merely a matter of days before the new owners arrived. A car-full of them: an elderly man, a younger woman and two children. They unpacked the car, which didn't take long as there were merely six suitcases and there they stood and marvelled at their new home, indeed they had the distinct appearance of a more Caribbean, than British family. ...

But then, thought Ted, what is British now? Only a few years ago in that survey they did, almost 95% of the population had classed themselves as "white". Why hadn't they asked if they classed themselves as British – that would have been much more interesting. Maybe they did and I just didn't get it. Whatever, a British passport nowadays doesn't necessarily mean one is really, and truly, British, does it? Ted looked over at Meg who had just closed her book, giving the signal she was ready for bed. Yes, he was, too.

7
The World Turned Upside Down

'I'll be off, then,' shouted Meg, 'Bernie isn't due to come for another two hours, so I'll be back way before he gets here!' She slammed the front door behind her, not waiting for an answer. Ted had been in a funny mood since they got up this morning. She assumed it was because he would have preferred to go with her to the cemetery and was angry with himself that he couldn't. Whatever the reason, she had no time for such nonsense. He was settled in the armchair, had a book and a cup of tea. That would have to suffice until she got back.

Ah, a Bernie day. Ted had forgotten about that. Bernie was a godsend. He could turn his hand to just about anything. Anything needed repairing, Bernie could do it. No idea how much money he has saved us over the years, thought Ted. He paid him handsomely, of course; cash in hand every month, the last thing he wanted was to get on the wrong side of Bernie. Ted was angry with Meg for going off to the cemetery without him. Michael was his friend and he was missing him dearly. She could have waited. Chances were, he would be fit enough to go with her one day, just not at the moment. He felt deprived of energy, somehow drained. His legs were getting worse and he often had this funny sensation in his face, she could be a little more sympathetic, couldn't she? Ted picked up the book which Meg had left for him on the coffee table. Another Grisham! I've told her so many times, I don't want to read any more Grisham books. Does she ever really listen to me? he thought. He suddenly heard a car drive up – the new neighbours at Number 2. Ted studied them carefully. What a turn up for the book this was. Who would have thought it? He closed his eyes – and fell asleep.

He awoke with a start to the sound of Bernie mowing the lawn in the front garden. He must have been asleep for almost two hours. Where was Meg?

The tea cup was still on the coffee table – stone cold – Bernie looked up and waved at him. He waved back and smiled. He knew Bernie would not leave without coming in for a chat.

If only he had sat in the wheelchair he could have, no he couldn't have. He was doomed to this until, well until he was ready to get a grip on himself. He had to admit it, sometimes he did overdo the helplessness, he sometimes could do more than he claimed he was capable of. Surely, that was understandable. If I once push myself too far, I'll be expected to do even more, won't I? And it was his burden to bear, after all.

Ted noticed Bernie signalling to someone – he couldn't see who – probably Meg – about time she got back. He heard the key in the lock, yes Meg. He could hear – who could he hear? It wasn't Meg. It was definitely two men and a woman, but not Meg. When they entered the living room Ted 's blood ran cold. This was definitely not going to be good news. Two police officers – one man and one woman entered the room with Bernie. The looks on their faces didn't really offer any hints as to why they were here but they weren't smiling. Ted could see their teeth, but it wasn't a smile. Bernie said, 'I'll go and make some tea for us all, shall I?' 'That's a lovely idea, thank you!' said the woman police officer. She introduced herself as WPC Barnes. She had a pleasant, very calm voice. PC Anderson also introduced himself and they both sat down – PC Anderson on the couch and WPC Barnes on the window sill. What a funny thing to do, thought Ted. Why would she sit on the window sill? The words which then came out of her mouth were barely understandable. They were muddled, murky, didn't make sense.

Then she said, 'Can we call someone to be with you?' 'Meg will be back soon,' said Ted.

'Sir,' she said, 'do you have any other relatives nearby?' 'Our daughter lives on the South coast. Not exactly nearby. They come up regularly, though. Our son is in Belgium on a business trip at the moment, he's due back next week.' 'What is your daughter's name, Sir?' 'Rosemary.' 'Do you have her telephone number somewhere?' 'It is in the telephone book next to the phone in the hall,' said Bernie who had just arrived with a tray of teacups. 'I'll get it for you.'

He returned within seconds, no one having said a word in his absence. 'Dolly's number is in here, too. I'll call her and ask her to come over. She is the carer who is looking after Ted at the moment. She lives just around the corner.' 'Thank you very much, Sir!'

The police officers stayed with Ted until Dolly arrived. The scene which had seemed so surreal to Ted up until then suddenly hit him. Dolly arrived with tears pouring down her cheeks. She sobbed uncontrollably as she walked into the room, said nothing just held Ted's hands in hers as she sank to her knees on the floor in front of him. Ted let loose, without any warning he screamed out loud, sunk back into the armchair and groaned as the tears rolled. His chest heaved fitfully. This was enough for the professional in Dolly to surface and take over. She stood up, dried her cheeks with the back of her right hand, stroked Ted's head with her left hand and reached for her bag. She had brought with her an injection which would calm Ted down for a while, sufficient time to get him into the wheelchair and to make the necessary phone calls. The woman police officer had tried to call Ted's daughter but there was no answer. Someone else should maybe deal with that now – Dolly felt she was the best option.

Bernie was in the kitchen wiping down surfaces and generally just passing time, idly wandering around the room, trying to assess the situation. He had been working for the Halloways for nearly 15 years now. Meg was such a lovely woman, always so thoughtful and compassionate.

When his wife, Daisy had fallen on the ice last winter she had taken over food every second day to ensure that they both got a hot meal and had done all the shopping for them for weeks. And now she was gone – what a shock! Only spoke to her yesterday, thought Bernie, and now, I'll never speak to her again. How am I going to tell Daisy? Then he realised this was all nothing compared to what Ted was going through. He just hoped that Rosemary could get up here quickly. She was such a caring daughter. She would surely be here by tomorrow.

He stared out of the window into the back garden, the garden which he could almost consider his own, he had put so much thought and effort into it. The tears ran down his cheeks as the police officers entered the kitchen. They were leaving now. Dolly was with Ted and she was in control of the situation. She would be staying with Ted until his daughter arrived. No matter how long that should take.

Ted dosed off, an uneasy, medication-enforced sleep encased him. Although all the pictures in his head were distorted and blurred, he knew it was Meg. She was trying to contact him. She wanted to tell him something but the words were not audible. He wanted to tell her something too but he couldn't open his mouth. He wanted to tell her that he loved her, always had done, from day one, and had never stopped. He wanted to tell her that he was proud of her, always had been. He wanted her to know he was suffering excruciating pain at her loss. There was a hole in his life – a hole he couldn't fill – indeed didn't want to fill. He wanted the hole – if he couldn't have her back, he wanted the hole.

When Dolly brought him some soup, he didn't want any soup. When Dolly brought him tea, he didn't want any tea. Dolly refused to bring him the photo album. He'd decided he'd get it himself once she went home. Dolly said she wasn't going home until Rosemary had arrived.

She would be here by tomorrow, around 2ish tomorrow afternoon. Ted could wait – he'd get it then. In the meantime, he had the pictures in his head, they were less blurry now. Meg had been such a beautiful bride, such a wonderful mother, such an adoring daughter, such caring daughter-in-law, such a wonderful wife. And now she was a corpse, lying cold in the hospital.

The doctor came after surgery had finished and expressed his sincerest condolences. Meg had been his patient for more than 30 years. He felt for Ted and felt with him in his loss. He gave him another injection to calm him down and gave Dolly instructions as to how many tablets he should be given and when. If there were any unforeseen difficulties, she should call his surgery and he would come round.

Dolly stayed with Ted. She wouldn't leave him until Rosemary had arrived – that is what she had told the police and that is what she intended to do. Her husband was at home at present and he could ensure everything ran smoothly at home until she got back. She had called the agency and explained that there was no alternative; she had to stay with Ted. The manager hadn't been too enthusiastic; it would mean re-arranging a number of schedules but she gave in, Dolly left her no choice.

The night was restless, both for Ted and Dolly. Ted kept waking and more than once called out for Meg. Dolly was in a very light sleep anyway, the couch in the living room was less than comfortable and she was on constant watch, always listening out for the slightest sound or movement from the room next door. Ted had been sleeping in the study for a number of weeks now, so much easier not to have to manage the stairs every morning and every night.

At 6:00 a. m. Dolly decided she would get up and prepare some breakfast. She needn't have bothered – Ted wasn't in the least bit interested in any of it. It took her all of her persuasive powers to get him to even drink anything, let alone eat. He claimed he couldn't stomach it. Claimed he would be sick all over the bedcover if she so much as placed the food under his nose.

This was going to be a long day but he would have to at least get up, get washed and dressed and settled in his wheelchair. Dolly was adamant, so Ted gave in. He stuck his heels in at sitting in the armchair in the bay window, though. That was too much to expect of him. Dolly knew she had to pick her battles well and thus gave in on that point. He was in the kitchen in the seating area, in the wheelchair, by 10:05 a.

m. They sat together in the kitchen and connected without a sound, spoke without words.

The doorbell rang and as Dolly walked towards the front door, she glanced at the clock on the hall wall – it was 10:24. Dolly was more than surprised, who was this? A man stood standing on the doorstep. He smiled at her, showing off his amazingly white teeth. Dolly smiled back, couldn't help herself, he had such a warm, embracing smile that it was difficult not to react. He introduced himself as Charles Riley, the new neighbour from opposite. Dolly glared at him as harshly as she could. She noticed the bible in his hand and asked, 'Are you a priest?' 'No, I'm not. And even if I were, I am here as a neighbour. To offer my condolences.' 'News travels fast, doesn't it? The accident only happened yesterday.' 'I just heard about it at the newsagent's and decided to waste no time.' 'Mr Halloway is not ready to receive visitors at the moment. I'll be sure to tell him you called, though.' Charles Riley was not one to take "no" for an answer. He was used to having his way and had a manner about him which certainly oozed with authority. He looked her straight in the eye, smiled, opened up his arms as if he were about to embrace her and simply said, 'I know he will receive me – let´s just go inside.' Dolly was taken aback and somehow found herself stepping aside and allowing the man to enter the hall. 'Follow me,' she heard herself saying.

It wasn't far to the kitchen at the back of the house, so she didn't have much time to decide how she was going to explain the presence of this strange man in the house. As she entered the kitchen, Ted looked up. 'There is someone here to see you,' she mumbled.

'I don't want to see anyone,' said Ted, he caught sight of the man behind Dolly, 'and certainly no one I don't even know. He must leave the house. He should come back and talk to Rosemary when she gets here, if it's something important.'

'But, I'm here to see you. To offer my sincerest condolences. I know what you are going through, my friend.' 'You have no idea what I am going through! Just leave me alone.' 'I have every idea – I went through it myself but ten months ago. I have not forgotten. How could I?' 'You're our new neighbour, aren't you? I recognise you now.' 'Indeed, I am, I moved in with my daughter-in-law and my two grandsons just a while ago.' 'Listen, I'm not in the mood for polite introductions and damned small talk. Just let me be, go away. We'll talk some other time. And another thing, we won't be needing that bible you're clutching. God has played his hand and I don't appreciate it. Now leave.' 'I felt very bitter when my wife died – just as you do now. I was angry with everyone else who was still alive and I questioned God's presence, his decision, questioned even if it were just that she should be gone and others lived on.' Charles Riley fetched a chair from the kitchen table and placed it close to Ted. He sat down on it and looked Ted deep in the eyes. 'Tell me, what was your wife like?' Ted closed his eyes – Dolly wasn't sure how he was going to react, she held her breath and looked out of the window – merely so as not to have to face the situation.

When she turned her head back, a sincere smile filled her face.

Charles Riley was holding Ted's hands in his, leaning forward and listening intensely to what Ted was saying. Ted was describing Meg, telling him how she had braved so many storms and how she had always been his one true love. How she had always been there for him and for the children. How she had made this house their home, a loving home. He wasn't crying, there were no tears in his eyes. It was as if he were simply revealing his feeling of pride in his wife and her achievements. Dolly listened for a while and then suddenly felt overwhelmed by a sense of being superfluous. No, not just one too many in the room, she actually was not needed right now, right here. She left the kitchen and went into the living room where she lay down on the couch where she had spent the night and fell asleep within seconds.

She woke up to the sound of Charles Riley's voice from the kitchen door, saying, 'I'll see you tomorrow, then, Ted. I'll come at the same time as today.' He walked straight past the study door and she heard the front door fall into the lock.

She got up and walked the few paces to the kitchen where she saw Ted sitting, as she had left him but somehow different. She noticed that he had even allowed the bible to be left on the table – he had his right hand placed on the cover. As she didn't know what to say, she said nothing, merely went to the cupboard and got out some soup plates. Surely he would take some soup today. Was worth a try, at least.

Ted did accept the soup and the tea which was offered. He also thanked Dolly for being with him. There was a serenity enveloping him which seemed almost unreal, Dolly wasn't inclined to spoil the aura. She was literally urging time to pass till Rosemary arrived and she could leave. It wasn't that she didn't feel for Ted, or that she didn't feel a loss regarding Meg, but she needed to go home – hold her husband and her children in her arms, thank God for their presence and come to terms with the event that had so suddenly and unrepentantly struck this patient. She willingly helped Ted into his bed after lunch. He said he wished to sleep a while, so he would be more alert when Rosemary arrived. He made her promise to wake him.

8
The World Keeps Turning

Rosemary arrived at quarter to three. The journey had been horrendous. Since the introduction of compulsory seat belts (almost 14 years ago in 1983) she hated long journeys. She hated the fact that she was confined and felt as if she could get no breath and to top it all, she had forgotten the wooden clothes peg. The clothes peg was perfect to ensure the belt wasn't too tight.

There was a pile-up on the motorway due to a car accident and she had been stuck in the traffic jam for what seemed like unending hours. Hours which had seen her sitting alone in her car, with her mind racing and her thoughts jumbled. How on earth was she going to manage all that was about to be placed on her shoulders?

She had spoken to Ian. It had been a short phone call – he didn't have time, he said, for a longer conversation. Even when he knew what she was calling about – their mother had been involved in a fatal accident – he wouldn't speak to her. He had agreed to travel back early, he would try to get a flight for Saturday morning and he would travel directly to their parents' house. He would meet her there. Rosemary had been so shocked to experience her brother in such a light but she hadn't plucked up the courage to disagree, or comment on anything. Just accepted all he said and agreed to meet him at Dad's at the weekend. She revisited the call over and over again in the traffic jam. What was wrong with him? Then she remembered that she hadn't spoken to her father yet. Was she doing the same thing as Ian? Was she in denial? No, she wasn't. She had spoken to Dolly four times over the afternoon and evening. She had ensured her father was well-cared for and that he would manage until she got there. She had cancelled all her appointments for today, in fact for today and all next week – and she had packed her suitcase and set off first thing this morning.

She was not, she had to admit it, easy with the situation. She had hardly spoken to her husband. He had held her tight and caressed her hair but she had pulled away. She didn't feel comfortable with such emotions.

Maybe that was what Ian was fighting with – emotions, or rather the lack of them – more to the point, the lack of the ability to release them, accept them, show them. That was maybe the Halloway gene. She dreaded seeing her father. How was he coping? How were they going to cope with helping him cope? She could foresee her and her family being saddled with looking after Ted. Ian would probably hide behind his job, claim he couldn't possibly be expected to be hands-on but he would pay his share of any costs which would be incurred. That would leave her to sort things out. She didn't feel up to it, by any stretch of the imagination. She couldn't begin to imagine what it would be like to have her father living with them, not that they didn't have the space, but the time. The time factor would be the knock-out.

She stopped for a break around lunch time, she wasn't hungry, she simply needed to brace herself for the situation at the house. It was therefore shortly before three by the time she arrived in Empire Close. She pulled into the driveway, switched off the engine, unbuckled her seatbelt, grabbed the steering wheel with both hands and tensed. She opened the car door and got out, walked over to the front door and rang the bell. She had a key, she had a key with her, but rang the doorbell anyway – just as she always did when they came to visit.

A car drove by, heading up the Close but Rosemary didn't look to see who it was. She waited – Dolly came to the door and let her in. Once the front door was closed, they embraced and held each other tight for a number of seconds. Rosemary wasn't sure if this was helping her but Dolly seemed to need it. The two women went into the kitchen and Dolly put the kettle on. 'Where is Dad?' asked Rosemary. 'Is he in the study?'

'Yes, he went for a lie-down after lunch and said I was to wake him when you arrived. I have been checking on him regularly, he has slept well. He didn't have a good night, as you can imagine.' 'Let's not wake him. Sleep will do him good.' She had hardly said the words when she realised how stupid they were – he wasn't ill, well that was not what was defining his condition at the moment. Sleep was not going to heal what he was going through. It struck her just how out of her depth she was here.

They drank their tea and discussed how they would manage the next few days. Who would do what, who would speak to whom, who would answer the phone, who would do the shopping. Funny, Rosemary thought, we haven't even written Ian's name down once yet and the list is already quite long. He would have to undertake to supervise the funeral arrangements. That in itself was a huge chunk. Rosemary realised she was going to have to speak quite openly with her father about all sorts of things that had never been communicated over the years. Did he want a cremation? Or rather, had Mum wanted to be cremated? She didn't know. She hoped her father did.

Dolly said she would go and get some groceries in for the weekend and would then go home but she could come back in the morning if that was what Rosemary wanted. She expressed as diplomatically as she felt she could, that Ted could actually be pushed to do a little more than he wanted. Obviously, he was in need of help and she was there to help but he shouldn't be fussed. She would come and get Ted up and about in the morning, while Rosemary dealt with whatever else needed to be done, if that was OK with Rosemary. Dolly purposely avoided spelling out what needed to be done: someone had to go to the hospital, someone had to contact the funeral directors, someone had to make decisions. It should be Ted, of course. Together with his children, if that was what he wanted.

Dolly left for the shops and Rosemary opened the door to the study. Her father was still fast asleep, so she walked over to the bed and looked at him, peacefully asleep. Tears filled her eyes, she wiped them away with the back of her hand but they kept coming, a seemingly never-ending flow.

The doorbell rang. Rosemary dried her eyes with her sleeve and paced towards the front door. Through the pane she could roughly see the outline of two people, in black. 'Oh no, not condolence visits already. I can't take this,' she thought. But it was too late, the people outside had already become aware that someone was home. Rosemary opened the door and found herself staring into the eyes of her first great love: Matteo. She would recognise that face anywhere – even after all this time.

She had had such a crush on him as a teenager, would sit in her bedroom upstairs and hope to be able to catch a glimpse of him walking past. They weren't at school together as she and Ian went to the independent school and Matteo attended the state school, which was much closer to the Close – and, if Rosemary remembered correctly – was where the best-looking boys were. She had never had the courage to speak to him, had merely loved from afar, until it dwindled away and fell to dust. Now, here he stood with what must be his mother, Caterina. It was him who spoke. 'We are so sorry for your loss. Please accept our sincerest condolences. My mother has cooked some casserole for you. May it warm you inside and help you through this difficult time.' Caterina held out her hands and when Rosemary made a gesture to shake it, Caterina held her hand between her two palms and closed her eyes. She was obviously praying, so Rosemary did not wish to interrupt, all the same she felt uncomfortable. She hardly knew these neighbours and here they were on her doorstep, praying for her, or with her, she didn't quite know which. 'Caterina remembers how she felt when my father died, she knows what it means to mourn someone so close. She wishes you to know that she will bring you food, if you need it. Please accept our help.' Rosemary was moved by the way Matteo spoke. His gentle voice with the stark Italian accent was, well, soothing, if not sexy. 'Thank you so much. I greatly appreciate it – as will my father. He is sleeping at the moment, so I can't ask you in.'

'No problem. Here is a basket with some fruit. I have put a note in with our phone number. Please call when you need help. Your father is ill himself, is he not? You will need help. We are there for you. We will never forget what your mother did for us, especially for my mother.' 'Thank you!' was all Rosemary could think to say. She was overwhelmed by the sincerity of Matteo's words and the sorrowful look in his mother's eyes. They turned and walked back down the pathway, Matteo holding his mother by the arm. Rosemary turned around and carried the casserole dish into the kitchen, then returned to pick up the basket of fruit which was still standing on the doorstep. As she slowly closed the front door, she heard her father's voice. He was calling for Dolly. Rosemary felt a pang of, what was it, jealousy? Then she remembered that her father did not know yet that she was here. She went into the study to greet him.

'Oh, it is you,' he said. 'Yes, Dad. Here I am.' 'That's good.' 'Ian will be coming soon, as well.' 'Good, good,' there was a long pause within which Ted tried to sit up more straight but he gave up and just said, 'I can't handle this, Rosie.' 'We'll manage, Dad.' She wanted so much just to hold him, embrace him but something was holding her back. 'Who was at the door?' asked Ted. 'Was it Dolly, has she gone home?' 'No. Dolly's gone to get some groceries for us. It was the next-door neighbours – Big Joe's family. They brought round some casserole and some fruit.' 'That's nice of them. I can't eat it, though. Can't keep the food down, you know. Don't want to.'

'Do you want to get up, Dad?' asked Rosemary. 'Yes, but Dolly can help me when she gets back. She knows what to do. She's very good. I don't know what I would do without her.' Rosemary felt another pang. 'OK, I'll make us some tea in the meantime then.'

She was performing this task when she heard the key in the lock, heard the door open, someone placing bags on the hall floor, closing the door, picking up the bags, walking towards the kitchen – she almost found herself imagining that her mother would enter the kitchen.

Naturally, it wasn't – it was Dolly. 'Something smells good, Rosemary. Have you been cooking?'

'No, our next-door neighbours brought round some casserole and some fruit.' 'That's nice of them. Did your Dad agree to see them? Or did he put up the defences?' 'He was still asleep, so neither I, nor he had to make that decision.' 'Is he still in bed?' 'Yes. He wanted to wait for you to help him get up.'

'Right, I'll go in to see to it. But you do know that I am then leaving, don't you?' 'Yes, that's fine. You have already done so much. I am extremely grateful.'

Rosemary put away the grocery shopping and finished making the tea while Dolly got Ted settled in the front room. He was in his wheelchair, so he could be relatively mobile – if he wanted to be – which remained to be seen.

They all sat in more or less silence as they drank their tea. Simple comments on the heat of the tea, or the window showing up the fact that it hadn't been cleaned for a while, was all that passed between them. Then Dolly said, 'Right, I should be going now. Ted, I'll come back tomorrow morning. Is 10ish, OK?' 'Maybe 9:30 would be better. Charles Riley is coming over again tomorrow. He said he'd come at 10:30 – like today.' Rosemary looked surprised. 'Who's Charles Riley, Dad?'

'He's the new fellow in Michael's house, across the way.' Rosemary's surprise did not disappear. 'I didn't realise you knew him so well.' 'I don't, I only met him today. But he's coming over tomorrow at ten thirty, like I said.' Dolly stood up – she knew only too well that they weren't such good acquaintances but she knew when to say nothing.

Rosemary escorted Dolly to the door and remained in the hall to make the telephone calls she had been putting off since she arrived. She needed to make appointments at the hospital and with the police. She'd speak to Ian about the funeral directors later.

9
Number One, Empire Close

Saturday morning came, of course it did. And along with it came Dolly. Rosemary was so glad that she had this help. It had been so difficult getting her father to bed the evening before. He was so stubborn. Conversation had been sparse too. Somehow, he didn't seem to want to talk at all. Rosemary had gone to bed early but had slept badly, uneasy in the thought that she had to accept the fact that she wasn't that close to her father. They had never argued, never fallen out – but, simply not close. Not as a father and daughter should be. What was the problem? She couldn't say, couldn't say because she had only just become aware of it. All her life she had assumed that their relationship was "normal", now she realised that it was strained, was that normal? Her relationship with her mother had undoubtedly been better but she had to accept that they had never spoken about some of the most important decisions which now would have to be made. Very probably her father would know her mother's wishes but would she be able to tell if he didn't adhere to them and decided for himself which was best? How could she even contemplate this thought? From what she knew of her mother she would want a church burial. No cremation, no big get-together after the ceremony and no flowers – she would have wanted people to give to charity. Dad would know which one. That was a conversation they would have to have once this "Charles Riley" had left. She was certainly intrigued about this chap.

Dolly got Ted up and ready for breakfast which they all ate together in the kitchen. Rosemary then wheeled her father into the front room where he said he wanted to sit in peace. At 10:30, on the dot, the doorbell rang – it was Charles Riley.

Rosemary was surprised when she saw him, in fact she had to check herself and just managed to hide her irritation – somehow the man's obvious non-British background caught her unawares – or was it more that she thought the man's appearance was non-British, whatever it was, it unsettled her. They shook hands. 'My father is expecting you, Mr Riley.' 'Oh please call me Charles – Charles Riley. That's what I'm used to. Everyone on the island called me Charles Riley.' 'What island would that be, Charles Riley?' 'Why, Monserrat. Did your father not mention it?' 'No, no he didn't, must have slipped his mind.' What had she heard about Monserrat? There was something, what was it? They entered the front room. 'Dad. Charles Riley is here to see you.' 'Do come in, Charles Riley. I am pleased to see you.' 'My, what a wonderful view of the Close you have from here, Ted. Lovely!'

Rosemary thought she had already outstayed her welcome and retreated to the kitchen. 'What the hell?' she said to Dolly, who simply shrugged her shoulders and picked up her coat and bag to leave. 'I'll drop in again this evening then around 9:00 p. m. if that's OK.' 'Yes, great. Thanks, Dolly. Oh, Dolly, I don't suppose you could sit with Dad this afternoon for a couple of hours could you? I have to go to the hospital and to the police station. I've got appointments at three and at four. Ian won't be here until tomorrow.' 'Oh, OK. Sure. I'll come back by half past two. You go and get things sorted. Don't worry about things here.'

Rosemary sat down, she didn't bother to show Dolly out, she knew the way. She needn't have bothered to sit down though, for she heard voices from the hall and immediately had to get back up again to see what the commotion was. Dolly had encountered two people at the door.

Rosemary recognised them as the neighbours from the end of the Close – the Nowaks. They were both dressed in black and the husband bore a gift basket full of meats and cheeses. 'Mr Nowak, how kind of you.' she said. 'We heard the news yesterday and wish to offer our sincerest condolences to you and your family. 'Mrs Nowak nodded in agreement and let her head sink. She then looked up and offered the birch branches which she was carrying to Rosemary. The look which she got must have made her realise that Rosemary was not quite sure what to do with the branches. 'They are for the door,' she offered as explanation. 'Thank you both so much!' Rosemary felt rather awkward standing with them on the doorstep like this but she didn't feel she could invite them in – she somehow felt her father would not take kindly to being interrupted. 'How is Mr Halloway? – it must be very bad for him, especially as he is in a wheelchair himself at the moment,' asked Mr Nowak. 'He is taking it rather badly, I'm afraid. I can't ask you in. Please do not be offended. Things are very difficult at the moment.' 'We understand completely. If you need anything, please do call us, or just come up to the house and let us know. We are very happy to help wherever we can. We want you to know that.

We will never forget how your dear mother helped us out.' 'Thank you very much. I do appreciate it.' With that Mr and Mrs Nowak walked back down the path and headed towards their home and Rosemary placed the birch branches on the hall table and walked back to the kitchen with the basket in her arms. She made herself a further cup of tea and drank it, feeling alone, distressed and helpless at the kitchen table of her parents' house. If only Ian were already here – they weren't that close but at least he would be able to share the burden.

Rosemary popped her head around the door to the front room, the atmosphere was extremely relaxed and the two men were in conversation as if they were old school friends. Rosemary left them to it and went upstairs to make her bed. She had slept in her old bedroom and when she entered the room, she suddenly felt like a small child again. The rosettes still hung on the pin board next to her bed and the certificates of past glories still hung on the walls, framed as trophies, by her proud parents. If only Ron were here with her. She'd call him after lunch and see if he could take time off and come up to help her. The children could maybe stay at friends. It would make such a difference. She sat down on the bed and … the doorbell rang again. She went back downstairs and opened the door to find two more neighbours standing on the doorstep. She recognised them as the Almons from Number 4. 'Sarah and I wish to offer our sincerest condolences on your loss,' said Mr Almon. 'I know you will excuse that we couldn't come yesterday. We wish you to know that we will help in any way wished. We will never forget how your mother helped us when we were in need and we are here for you now. Please feel free to call.' His wife smiled at Rosemary and held both her hands in her own, she pressed them slightly and Rosemary felt a slight teardrop fall on the back of her hand.

The sincerity was overwhelming. 'Thank you so much. We will definitely contact you if we need anything, or when more details of the funeral are arranged. Thank you!'

The pair handed Rosemary an envelope enframed in black, matching the black ribbon which each were wearing on their sleeves. They turned and went away, slowly and without looking back.

As Rosemary stood watching them depart, she looked up at the sky and saw only blue, not a cloud to be seen. 'Are you up there, Mum? Are you watching us? Are you checking if we get all this right?' She looked down at the ground beneath her and noticed that some weeding needed to be done. She must have a word with Bernie about that.

With that thought she turned, closed the front door and walked towards the kitchen. She didn't get far, as she passed the living room door her father called out to her, 'Rosie, would you see Charles Riley out.'

'Sure,' she replied. She put the card down on the hall table and signalled to Charles Riley to step ahead of her. She was so curious about this man; dare she ask him questions? 'Thank you for spending time with my father. It seems to be doing him a world of good.' 'I am deeply moved that he should recognise a soul mate in my humble self. I too lost my wife just a few months ago. He knows that I can relate to his intense pain, he rests assured that we can imagine each other's inner torment and he trusts that we can find courage together to master what is before us.' They had reached the door and Rosemary opened it. As Charles Riley walked through it, he turned and said, 'I will return tomorrow at the same time.

Good day, Mrs Rosie.' 'Yes, a good day to you also, Mr Riley.'

Ted thought he could maybe manage some lunch today and wheeled himself into the kitchen. Rosemary suggested the casserole which Matteo and Caterina had brought over. She would heat it up. With that thought – came three others – what did they mean by saying Mum had helped them so much? And what did the Nowaks mean? And what did the Almons mean? She had no idea. 'Dad, we have had two more visitors at the door this morning. The Nowaks and the Almons. They brought cards, I'll show you. Did you see the card from Caterina?' 'Yes. I have put it on the mantelpiece in the front room. Such kind words. So grateful. I don't know what for but they are very grateful.' Rosemary handed him the other two cards which he duly opened and read. 'They are grateful, too, they don't say what for, either. Put them with the others will you, Rosie.' At that moment, the post popped through the letterbox. There were seven cards in all, news travels fast in such towns as this.

They could all be read after lunch, Rosemary was glad her father was willing to try and eat something warm – she didn't want to wait too long, he may change his mind. During lunch she carefully approached a subject which was weighing on her mind. 'Dad, which Funeral Directors do you think I should call?' 'We'll take the Hammonds from Leighton Lane. They were very good with both Grandma and Grandpa.' 'That was a while ago, Dad, like 20 years.' 'What was good enough then, is good enough now.' 'It could have changed hands.' 'They have a good reputation, good solid family company. Might well be the lads running it now but they will have learnt the trade well from their father. We'll take them.' Rosemary didn't argue but did make a mental note that it would seem her father knew what he wanted and would put his foot down if necessary. Let's hope it won't be, she thought and finished the bowl of delicious casserole. She must remember to praise Caterina for that.

Ted went for a lie down after lunch and was still in bed when Dolly arrived to take over from Rosemary. He didn't want to get up but he did want to look at the cards which had arrived in the post.

Rosemary longed to have someone with her but it was not to be. Her husband, Ron had something he needed to deal with and Ian hadn't been able to get a Saturday flight. At the hospital she was able to see her mother in the morgue and was given papers which her father needed to sign in order for her to be able to be picked up by the funeral directors. At the police station it was only slightly better. Although it was not as bad as actually having to see her mother, she had to endure an exact description of the accident which had cost her mother her life. The lorry driver had overlooked her, plain and simple.

A pedestrian had exited the cemetery and was walking along the footpath to the west of the grounds when a lorry took the turning too fast and swerved to avoid a lamppost, not seeing that by doing this he was headed straight for the pedestrian. Meg Halloway died on her way to the hospital.

The lorry driver was in shock. Rosemary was, as well. The lorry driver was being treated in hospital. Rosemary was on her own and felt weighed down by responsibility. She signed the papers lying before her and left for home, shaking, shocked and angry.

Once home, she added "contact lawyer" to Ian's to do list which, she felt, was still much too short.

10
The Depths of Our Loved Ones

Rosemary was running late. She had promised Dolly that she would be back by 5:00 p. m. She had even gone so far as to say that if she weren't, then Dolly could go home anyway, she wouldn't be far away. After her last discussion with Dolly it had become more than obvious that her father could do much more than he let on. Dolly had been very diplomatic but also very professional. She had explained the curiosities of MS and the effect it has on the sufferers. She had been adamant that Rosemary could ask more of her father than he was presently professing to be able to do. If left alone for limited periods of time he would come round. He was equipped with a panic button which was activated in such a way as to first alarm anyone in the house, then any pre-determined person close by and/or the ambulance service. This lovely gadget could be our family's life-line as well as his, Rosemary had thought when she processed this idea in her mind.

Back at home she found her father still in the study, he was sitting in his wheelchair staring at the wall. As she joined him there, he suddenly proclaimed, 'You know what, Rosie, I never asked your mother what she did all day.' 'What do you mean?' 'When I got home in the evening, I never asked her what she had done all day. I thought it was better that way. I didn't want her to think I didn't notice if she had polished the stair banisters, or dusted all the ornaments in the living room.

I thought it was better not to ask.' 'Where is this coming from, Dad?' 'All these cards we are getting, everyone is so grateful to your mother for helping them – and I have no idea what she did.' 'Did she never say anything?' 'No. She would always ask how the day had been for me and if I was exhausted, or if we should go for a stroll together – usually around the common. More often than not, we went – I thought she had been indoors all day …' Ted had to stop, his emotions were overwhelming him again.

'We talked about all sorts of things; about buying a microwave oven, as they were so useful, or a video recorder, so we could watch videos with Michael and Mary, about Charles and Diana, how sad it is that they are separated. She never complained – even when I said we couldn't buy a new freezer immediately when the old one packed in. And, she was always content.' 'Dad, you shouldn't be doing this to yourself. You were a good husband. Mum adored you. You couldn't do anything wrong in her eyes.' 'That is exactly the point, isn't it? I was so busy enjoying the fact that she accepted anything I said, did, or even just thought, that I was completely oblivious to the fact that I didn't know what she actually did, or really thought.'

'Well, I hope you two managed to set out some kind of plans for the situation in which we, or rather you, find yourself now. I called Hammonds and they will be over to see you tomorrow morning at 11:30.' 'Thank you, Rosie!'

'Do you want me to be with you when they come?' Although it did seem funny asking the question, somehow Rosemary thought it needed to be articulated. 'Yes, sure. I'm fine with that. When will Ian be here? Will he be here in time for the meeting?' Rosemary hoped so, she sincerely hoped so, she didn't want to be left alone on this one – alone with her father. She wanted to ask him straight out, what his plans were, but for some reason, she felt she couldn't. Truth be known, she didn't want to know yet. The minute she knew it would mean she would have to start planning and arranging things and she was happy to have another night's sleep before starting on that.

Rosemary suggested a Chinese take-away for dinner. Ted had no objection but reminded her that he wasn't going to eat a lot, so she shouldn't order too much. That agreed on, Rosemary went into the kitchen, found the leaflet, picked the dishes and called up – she was told everything would be ready in 20 minutes, she needn't come and fetch the order – they would bring it to the house for her. They offered their condolences.

As she now no longer had to drive anywhere, she poured herself a stiff gin and tonic and laid the table. 22 minutes later, the doorbell rang. Rosemary went to the door and was surprised to see two delivery men on the doorstep. They were both wearing black bands on their arm and both bowed as she greeted them. They offered their condolences and wished to express their sincerest of feelings for the mourning family. Rosemary thanked them, set the food on the hall table and opened her purse. The two men looked almost shocked, there was no way they were going to accept any money for the food. They were adamant. After all her mother had done for them, it was the least they could do to bring her family some food in these tormenting times. They hoped she and her father could enjoy the meal. With that they walked away, with their heads slightly down.

'Bloody hell, this is getting embarrassing,' thought Rosemary. 'My mother as Saint Theresa of Empire Close, or what!' She closed the door and forced herself to calm down, as she walked back to the kitchen to put the food on the table. On her way past the study she called to her father to come across and have his dinner. Accordingly, he wheeled himself into the kitchen. Good start, well – orchestrated, thought Rosemary, I'll build on that.

As they sat there at the table, it was almost a picture of a normal Saturday evening – two people eating their Chinese take-away, drinking their wine and chatting about this and that, but nothing really, except that it was father and daughter and not husband and wife. That would no longer be. Ted ate with a handsome appetite, he had not eaten properly since Thursday and actually he did feel slightly hungry – only his stomach didn't seem to want to play along. He hoped all would go well, and ate his portion. 'Did you have the food delivered, then? That's a new one. Your mother always went and got it.' 'Dad, they insisted.' 'Funny that.' 'It got even funnier.' 'What do you mean? Were they funny with you? You know I think they still don't speak proper English.'

'Their English was fine – and no, they weren't funny. They were sad, sad that Mum is gone.' 'They didn't even know her properly.' 'Seems they did, Dad. Seems they, too are also so grateful for all she did for them.' 'What? Are you kidding me, now? She didn't even know the Chinese family we have here in the Close, how would the Takeaway folks know her? I am not in the mood for jokes.' 'I'm serious. We both have no idea how much Mum was looked up to in the Close and in town, quite obviously.'

Ted had heard enough. He was lost in his thoughts and had no intention of furthering the conversation with his daughter. They sat in silence for the rest of the meal. Rosemary was not inclined to continue the conversation either. My goodness, she had so much which she wanted to ask about her mother but she knew her father knew no more than she did – at least when it came to her relationship with their neighbours in the Close.

Fortunately for Rosemary, Dolly came a little early to get Ted ready for bed. She was planning to go out with her husband and hoped it was OK with the two of them. She would be back at the normal time the next day for the morning ritual. Rosemary was only too pleased – she needed some time to herself. She had a lot to put into perspective and she wanted to do it before her brother arrived. She wanted to be able to present him with facts, at least facts as she could assess them and not just with this feeling of consternation which she currently felt when she started thinking of her mother and her mother's life here in the Close.

With Ted safely tucked up in bed by 9:30 p. m. Rosemary was free to a) call home, b) peruse the family photo album which she had found lying on the sideboard in the living room and c) gather her thoughts and calm her mind. The third aspect was becoming increasingly important as Rosemary was being haunted by an ever-growing idea that she had been an inattentive, if not disinterested, daughter.

11
Decisive Moves

Rosemary would have easily classed Charles Riley's visit on the Sunday morning as run-of-the-mill and uneventful, if it weren't for the meeting they had with the Hammonds afterwards. He had arrived punctually and gone straight into the study to talk with her father. She was left drinking tea with Dolly in the kitchen and was still to be found there when her brother arrived at 11:00. They didn't disturb their father for a while but then around 11:15 they decided that actually, it was Charles Riley who was going to have to take a back seat and he should leave to give them time with their father. They walked to the study and just as Ian put his hand on the door handle, the door opened and out walked Charles Riley. He paid his respects to Ian and proceeded to leave the house without further ado. Ian couldn't believe his eyes.

'What the hell?' he said as he walked in and greeted his father.

'Good to see you, Ian. Thank you for coming back early from your trip.' 'There was no question about it, Dad.' 'Dad, the Hammonds will be here in a minute. Should we talk about your plans before they arrive?' 'No, no need for that it's all quite simple really. We'll be done in a brace of shakes.' 'No, they need all sorts of details, Dad.' 'Like coffins, cards, charities, the funeral, speakers,' Rosemary was stopped in her tracks by a swift gesture of her father's right hand. 'Stop, right there,' he said but before he could go on further the doorbell rang. It was the Hammond brothers.

Ted was wheeled into the front room and they all sat down.

'Our condolences on your loss, Ted,' said the elder of the two, the younger nodded. 'Thank you,' said Ted. 'To you both as well,' he continued in the direction of Rosemary and Ian. 'It is a distressing time for all.' 'Have you been in touch with the hospital?' asked Ted. 'Indeed, we have. We are free to collect your Meg tomorrow morning and will take her to our premises. Assuming that is your wish, Ted.' 'Yes, it is. That's fine.' 'Will you be wanting a service similar to your Mum and Dad's?' 'No, we won't,' spurted out Ted, rather too quickly. 'Very quiet, only the closest family in the commemoration hall at the cemetery. Can you arrange that?' 'Indeed, we can.' Rosemary and Ian sat and listened, unsure whether to interrupt their father, or not. They looked at each other, questioning each other without words. Then suddenly Ian said, 'Rosie, why didn't you tell me?' 'Because I didn't know!' 'Dad, what's going on here?' 'Just leave it to me, you two. We can have a simple service with a short speech and a prayer and we'll quietly say our farewells to your Mum, to my Meg.' 'Dad, this is not what Mum would have wanted.' 'How do you know? Did you speak to her about it?' 'Well, no, but I'm sure she would have wanted a church service and a graveyard ceremony.' 'So, you don't know, then.' 'Dad, did you speak to her about it?' asked Ian. 'I didn't know she would be leaving me so soon, did I?'

Joshua Hammond, no newcomer to such scenarios, asked whether they should return later in the day.

'That won't be necessary, Josh.' Ted was adamant. 'We can fix all the details here and now. Be fair, you two. It has to be my decision and it is hard enough to say good-bye. I don´t want to have a great rigmarole just to please some of the ladies at the foodbank.'

'I can accept that, Dad, but maybe we should go through this together. We can find a compromise – something between a rigmarole and such an incredibly intimate send-off.' Ian was trying hard to stay calm. He could see that his sister was far from it. 'I would like her cremated, Josh.' said Ted. At this Rosemary left the room. She could take no more. 'If you're sure that is what you want, Ted.' 'I'm sure. And what's more I would like to have the farewell service this week. How soon can you arrange everything?' 'Dad, come on. Slow down.' 'Ian, please. You have to understand me. I need to do this my way. It is hard enough for me to say good-bye and I can't bear the thought of dragging this part of it on for ages – and just so that any number of people can come and attend a grand funeral service. Please stand by me.'

Ian was touched by the sound of his father's voice and by the words he had just heard, by the will and the strength which he could perceive. 'OK, we do it your way. I'll speak to Rosemary.'

'How soon can you arrange everything, Josh?' Ted repeated his question. 'Well, we'll need a speaker. I'll have to see who is available at short notice.' 'I have a speaker,' said Ted. 'I'll give you his name and telephone number. He is available any day this week.'

Ian was speechless. It was his turn to leave the room but he made a conscious attempt to show that it was not in disgust, more in despair.

Rosemary was upstairs in their parents' bedroom. She entered the room, collywobbles and sniffles, galore. She eyed the sewing machine next to the wardrobe and conjured up scenes of her mother sitting there busily sewing away, mending, altering, or even designing skirts and dresses. Rosemary had always been proud of her mother's creations, they had sometimes been slightly extravagant but had deemed her star of the show on many a festive occasion.

She was sitting on the bed with her face in her hands when Ian walked into the room and sat next to her. He put his arms around her and simply said, 'He has to do it his way. We have to respect that, Rosie.'

Rosemary didn't have the strength to contradict. This was all proving too much for her. She had not only lost her mother, she had lost her too early. Lost her before she had time to talk to her – woman to woman. Worst of all, was the gnawing fact that there had been plenty of time for such conversations, just no inclination for intimate discussions with her mother. And now it was too late.

Rosemary had no idea what her mother would have wanted, had no idea of who her mother really was. And now it was too late.

And so it was that there was a particularly intimate, intensely personal ceremony held for Margaret Theresa Halloway at 5:30 p. m. on Thursday in the commemoration hall at the cemetery. Her husband Ted, their children Rosemary, with husband, and Ian, plus wife were present. Her grandchildren were not there; they had remained at their respective homes in order to attend school. Charles Riley held a moving speech in celebration of the life of Meg Halloway and Josh Hammond and his brother were in attendance. The cremation was performed much later. No one was present.

The family went for a meal at The Wooden Spoon and it was there, over roasted duck with market vegetables and new potatoes, that Ted had something he wanted to inform them of.

12
A Change in Perception

It was a remote village pub but due to its location on the banks of the river it was very popular. As it was early evening the bar area was merely half full and the noise level was well-under what it would become later in the evening – even on a Thursday. The locals were a rowdy bunch and were known far beyond the boundaries of the village for their sing-a-long matches. Meg had loved it here and Ted felt close to her as he sat in the left corner at the table which they had come to refer to as "theirs". There were five of them around the table, so it was slightly cosy but Ted decided it was "intimate" and that was a good thing. The food was excellent – the resident cook was top notch.

Once they had all finished the main course and Mandy had collected the plates, Ted decided it was time. 'Charles Riley thought of the idea. He's arranging everything. We don´t have to do anything other than show up on Saturday afternoon.' 'But Dad …'

'No buts about it, I'm afraid. It´s all arranged. You will be here, won't you? That would be a slap in the face for the Close if you weren't here, Rosie. And you too, Ian, of course. Best would be for your family to be here, as well. And Ian's family. It is a Wake, after all. And it is for your mother.' 'I'm surprised you could decide all this without speaking to Ian and me about it first.' 'It was a fait accompli. Charles Riley did it,

I told you that.' 'That man hasn't even been in your life for two full weeks yet and he's already pushing you around. What is wrong with you?' 'Please, Rosie. We need to know, don't we? We need to know what your mother did all those years. We need to know how she helped all those people, all those people that we hardly know. This will get everyone together and we shall find out.' With these words he broke down.

The tears poured down his face and he sobbed and sobbed and sobbed.

Rosemary took her father in her arms and held him close. She was so relieved that he was feeling the same as she was – guilty as she still felt about herself it was a great relief to know that she was not alone. Her father hadn't really dug too deep into the soul of her mother, either. She knew that now and felt instantly better. Better, if only in the sense that she was no longer alone. 'Of course, we'll be there. My family will all come. Ian?'

'Christ, Dad. You know how to put people on the spot, don't you?' 'Ian, please. This is important.' 'I need to know more about this Charles Riley first. I just don't get it – what kind of a hold does he have on you?' 'He has no hold on me, he's a friend.' 'Dad, come off it. He's been in the Close for not even three weeks. You didn't know him from Adam before that. And, let's face it, he's not the type of person you would normally have as a friend, is he?' 'Ian, you're being nasty.' 'No, I'm being honest. 'Bout time somebody was.'

Ted took a deep breath; he knew he owed it to his children although something inside him was resisting with the argument that it was his choice who he defined as his friend. Be that as it may, it seemed they were not going to let him get away with not coming clean in some way. Ted declared

Charles Riley his manna from heaven. He proceeded to admit not wanting to see him at first – for he was the reason Meg was dead. Meg had been at the cemetery to tell Michael who his children had sold the house to.

Rosemary and Ian both looked in disbelief, their mother had been wanting to talk to a dead man – in his grave? This was beyond them.

Ted smiled as he interpreted the look on their faces. 'Yes, that was your mother. But the worst part is – it was unnecessary.' 'Spot on, Dad.' 'No, it was unnecessary because Michael would have done exactly the same. Charles Riley is a distant relative. Michael's great-great grandfather's brother left Ireland for Monserrat all those years ago. Left behind the family and never returned. He made a name for himself on the island, was respected and amassed an amount of wealth of which he was duly proud. Charles Riley had been searching through old manuscripts and papers, diving into the depths of the internet to reconstruct his family tree. He had written a letter to Michael just weeks before he died. Michael had been over the moon and they were planning a re-union – which never came to be. Two disasters struck: the volcano erupted and Michael died.'

'All very interesting – but it doesn't explain your express friendship, does it? Dad, come on. You'll have to give us more.'

'When the police came with the message about your mother, I was in denial for a few hours. I swear, just a few hours. I didn't want it to be true. Dolly gave me some medication to keep me calm, I'm sure that didn't really help me accept the truth but it did keep me calm. Next day, Charles Riley arrived at the door. Uninvited and bossy. Wouldn't take "no" for an answer. Just walked into my life and then just listened to me talking about Meg. Listened to me talking about our life, our family, our love. He knows things I hadn't even realised myself until I heard myself saying them. He is the most understanding person around. He can listen, understand and feel with you. He knows how to show compassion, he accepts emotions as they are and for what they are. I showed him photos of us – the whole family. I told him about Meg's illnesses and her triumphs, about her temperament and joyfulness.

Then came the hardest part, he forced me to accept that she had some failings, some parts of her character which I didn't like. That was difficult but it was a necessary part of the whole process.

That's what Charles Riley said, he said I mustn't turn her into a saint. I must remember her as she was – with all the good and bad bits. And that is what I am doing. She is part of my life still, although she is not here with us. She always was up until now and will remain firmly in my memory as what she was – My Meg.'

'Our mother, Dad.' Rosemary couldn't help herself, she squeezed Ron's hand. 'We are mourning too. Why couldn't you talk to me about her? I would have listened. I would have understood. Why someone from outside? I don't get it.'

'I didn't want to burden you.'

'You burdened me by not talking. You made me realise how emotionally distanced we are.' Tears poured down her face. Ron put his arms around her shoulder and glared at his father-in-law.

'I'm sorry!' was all Ted could say.

Ian could understand his father. He imagined he could act similarly in such a situation. He was naturally confused now as to whether this was the right way forward, or not, but he could follow the steps and acknowledge them as something acceptable – well, after Rosie's outburst maybe not quite acceptable but certainly viable. He looked at his wife, Anita. She was crying quietly; Ian knew this meant they would have to thrash this out at home. He wasn't going to get away with anything less than a commitment to be different to his father, that much was clear. Then he recollected what Ted had said before he started on his declaration of mourning; he had said they should all meet up with the neighbours in the Close to find out what Mum had done throughout all those years. Yes, those were his words. 'Dad, what aren't you telling us here? There is more, isn't there?'

'No, that's the whole Charles Riley story. I really didn't know him before he came to the Close.'

'I mean about mum. What did you mean by needing to know what she did all those years?' 'This is all very difficult for me. Trying to keep up the façade of strength. Rosie, you tell him.'

Ian looked puzzled. What did Rosie know that he didn't?

Rosemary began, 'We have had visitors to the house, offering condolences and bringing gifts. They all say how grateful they are to Mum for all the things she did for them.' 'That's what people say, when someone dies. Why are you hanging this up so high?' 'No, it is more than that. You didn't see these people. You didn't hear the sincerity in their words, in their voices. There is definitely more to it. Neither dad, nor I, know what. We need to find out.'

'Dad, surely you must have talked to mum about what she did while you were at work. How she was feeling, what she wanted to do, that sort of thing.'

For some reason he then looked at Anita, who had a somewhat pensive face, he knew then – they were going to have to do an awful lot more talking when they got home. He obviously was more like his father than he had ever dreamt.

Ian simply nodded his head, took a sip of his beer and stared into the horizon, which wasn't a horizon at all, it was the bar area of a local pub. For Ian, though, it could have been anywhere. He was overpowered by his thoughts. It was a hard lesson he was being taught in such a by-the-by manner. He had never questioned his relationship to his father, or his mother. They were his parents and they had been there for him as a child and as an adolescent. They had helped him through school and had supported him through university. They had cheered him on during his short spat as a local football hero. They had been thrilled when he told them he was getting married and they loved their grandchildren dearly.

They had never been indifferent but had never tried to persuade him against his will. They had instilled in him a feeling of being something special. And yes, they had encouraged him to stand up for his beliefs. His father had been a hard master, his mother a forgiving soul. He was the whip; she was the carrot. When he had graduated his father had shaken his hand and congratulated him, his mother had hugged him and kissed him on both cheeks. They were a steadfast in his life. But … were they content with their lives? Were they happy in their marriage? Were they financially sound? Did they vote to join the Common Market? He had no idea.

How could he possibly have been so absorbed by his life and his work that he hadn't found time out to be with them? And now it was too late. At least with regard to his mother but he still had time to alter things with his father.

Thus, when Saturday afternoon came, the complete Halloway family was gathered at Number One, Empire Close. Ted, Rosemary and Ron with their children, Alexander and Theresa, and Ian and Anita with their children, Alice and Paul.

As the hall clock struck 3:00 p. m. Rosemary pushed Ted in his wheelchair out of the front door and they headed to the centre of the Close where the neighbours were waiting for them. Ron, Ian and Anita were close behind them but the children were nowhere to be seen. After a lengthy discussion, in which neither Rosemary nor her father had seemed particularly interested in convincing the children to partake in the Wake, it had been decided that they could stay in the house and watch television, or a film. It was a relief to see that the welcoming committee in the road comprised also of the "older" generation: The Rileys from Number 2, the Amartis from Number 3, the Almons from Number 4, the Wangs from Number 5 and the Nowaks from Number 6.

13
The Wake

Charles Riley was obviously a good organiser. Everyone had been given a task and had excelled; it was a splendid show of hospitality, compassion and respect – a good send-off for a woman they all had come to admire. The long trestle table was covered with a black table cloth and at intervals down the table were white lilies in small white vases. There were garden chairs placed along the sides of the table and each had a black ribbon tied to the armrest. The food was laid out on separate tables. There was plenty of it and the variety was amazing. The plates were piled up on the right-hand corner, next to which was the cutlery – not the usual plastic and paper offerings of a street gathering, real china plates and proper cutlery. The serviettes were paper though and it wasn't until Rosemary took a closer look that she realised why. They were customised – printed on the serviettes was a photo of Meg, smiling as she always had been and spreading her positive aura. Under the photo was written: your place in our hearts is secured.

Once everyone had arrived, fetched something from the buffet and settled down to eat, Charles Riley stood up and said, 'We are gathered here to celebrate the life of Meg Halloway. Does anyone wish to say something?'

It was Matteo who stood up first. 'I wish to speak on behalf of my family. We, too had to deal with a death in the family – my father died some 15 years ago. He too was killed and was gone from one day to the next. It was a hard time for us all, so we know how you – the Halloways – are feeling now. But the reason we wish to participate in this celebration goes much deeper than just a common understanding of mourning a loved one. Meg Halloway had a big heart, was compassionate and a once-in-a-lifetime kind of neighbour.

After the death of my father, we (the children) both needed to get back to the routine of our individual lives. My mother fell into a huge hole. She had immense problems dealing with everyday situations. She had no one in the house to help her. No one to listen to her, no one to talk to her, no one to understand how she was feeling and suffering. But she did have Meg. Meg would come every morning and sit with her, or sew with her, or work in the garden with her. She was the one who brought us our mother back. She was the one who took the time out to show to our mother that life was worth living, even without the man you loved and even in a country which you didn't feel at home in, a country so cold and rainy and so unlike her beloved home region. Meg saved her from becoming an emotional wreck. It was Meg who suggested I move in with my family, that we form a family unit here. With that she saved us all. This is all fifteen years ago, as I said. But even to this very year, these two women had a strong bond. They were the closest of friends and would talk about everything to each other. They were confidantes in the most sincerest form. I speak for my mother when I say, Thank you. You will be missed greatly. Let us please raise our glasses once more to our neighbour – Meg.'

Ted had had no idea of any of this and he felt rather ashamed. Then he realised, that actually he should have known it, he should have anticipated it. He knew Meg, he knew what she was like and yes, that was her. He held up his glass and proudly toasted his wife.

Charles Riley asked, 'What is your home region like, Caterina?'

And she told them. She remained seated, firmly clutching her wine glass in her right hand and she described the flowing hills and the lush pastures of Tuscany. She spoke in fond tones of the vineyards and the woods, of the warm spring days, of the dry, hot summers and of the mild, rainy autumns and winters. Her face lit up when she recalled out aloud the mountain chains with few but fertile plains and never-ending rows of cypress trees. Tuscany – the home of world-best extra virgin olive oil, renowned as the breadbasket of Rome. Yes, she missed it, very much.

It was a while before Richard Nowak stood up. 'I speak for myself and for my wife, Madga, when I say we can underline every word Matteo has said about your wife, Ted. Meg was something special. Without her, we maybe would no longer be here – neither in Empire Close, nor indeed in England. My father was in the Polish Army and after its disbandment signed on with the Polish Resettlement Corps. It was to be for two years initially but at the end of that period he decided to accept the offer from the British Government and stay on. He went home to Poland only to fetch his childhood sweetheart. They married and returned to England. They were given British citizenship and their children, myself and my sister, were born here. We saw no reason to believe we were not British citizens. Everything went well until Magda and I wanted to get married. Suddenly, obscure paperwork was uncovered – paperwork which became more and more complex as time went on, climaxing in the registration of our new-born daughter. She was to be registered as Polish, born of Polish parents. We were in distress – until Meg took on the task of helping us. She had noticed Magda sitting on a bench on the common and realised she was crying. She sat down with her and Magda explained everything. Meg took it on herself to help us, she wrote to politicians and authorities. She called lawyers and lobbyists. She left no stone unturned until she had secured full British passports for both Magda, and myself and for little Maja. She rescued us. We, too, say Thank you to Meg. You will be greatly missed. Raise your glasses with us to Meg.'

Ted was speechless. He had no idea that Meg had done this. Why didn't she tell him? Did she think he wouldn't approve? How had she managed to keep it secret? How did she know who to contact? He had always known she was intelligent and knowledgeable, now he knew she could be persuasive, as well. His heart was overflowing, he was so proud of her. He held up his glass in response to the toast.

It was Charles Riley who again broke the calm as he asked, 'Which part of Poland did your ancestors come from?'

It was Magda who answered as Richard seemed quite drained by the recollections of how much Meg had actually helped them. Magda also remained seated as she spoke of the city of Bialystok. She noted that obviously no one knew quite where that was, so she explained it was in the province of Podlaskie (still no real recognition perceivable) in the Northeast of Poland on the border to Lithuania and Belarus (nods showed the audience was on track) Not wanting to let the side down and leave all the admiration in Italy, Magda spoke of the fields full of sunflowers, of the national park and the lush vegetation. Why maybe you know the famous forest of Bialowieza. But surely everyone knows Esperanto – it was created in Bialystok.

Rosemary and Ian had been silent throughout all of this and weren't really paying attention to the reminiscing of the two ladies. They, each for themselves, were delving deep into their souls and searching for memories of their mother. Not that there weren't any but they wanted to find memories that were in some way comparable to what they were hearing here. And they found them. There were numerous occasions where Ian had been able to turn to his mother for help, advice and comfort. He now realised he had filed them as "normal". After all, she was his mother. Of course, she was there for him. She had tucked him in at night, kissed the top of his head and always said, 'Sleep tight, darling,' it was always such a contrast to his father who would stand at the bedroom door and say, 'Good night, son.' As for Rosemary, she, too could recollect multiple situations where it had been her mother who had given her the strength, the self-confidence to attempt something. It was her mother who insisted she learn how to cook and sew for these were basic necessities for women in the world.

It was her mother who had been there when she had considered giving up show-jumping because she had not won a single prize all season. It was her mother who had comforted her when she had broken up with that awful boy, Jason. But then, she was her mother. Of course she had been there. Of course, she had helped. She had always come to say good night, had always tapped the blankets and said, 'Sleep well, life has plenty to throw at us tomorrow,' and once she had left the room, her father would come and say, 'Good night, my precious. Sleep well.' They were a well-oiled engine. A perfect team.

Isaac Almon stood up. 'For me it is extremely difficult to admit how we were helped by your mother (he looked at Rosemary and Ian), and your wife (looking at Ted), and indeed it is almost as embarrassing for my wife but it is a matter of honour that we should join you all in saluting the memory of Meg. 'Isaac Almon was genuinely suffering inside, he knew it was right to present the facts as they were but he struggled all the same. He continued in a subdued voice, almost a whisper, 'My parents are of Petticoat Lane origin and have created a chain of fashion stores from those humble beginnings. I, myself am Managing Director of the family firm. I mention this as I fear you will judge me harshly as my part in the tale I am to tell is not one of greatness. I was not there when Sarah needed me. Meg was. Meg was an observant woman and detected quickly that there was something amiss in our household. Sarah had given birth to our son and she struggled with the responsibility. She struggled also with herself, feeling she could not be the mother she should be to our son. It was this fear of having to admit her shortcomings, she did not confide in our religious community. She neglected the child – one day she had left him out in the front garden in the pram. This was to be our rescuing moment, for Meg saw this. She offered to take him for a walk. On return she spoke to Sarah and realised that there was a severe underlying problem.

She would take Salomon for walks every day after that, even care for him in her own home if on return she felt that Sarah was not quite ready. She never forced herself on us, on our home – she merely helped. It was almost four months before Sarah was ready to accept her full responsibilities. In all that time, Meg was there for her. In all that time, I had no idea. I learned of all this much later, when Sarah's feeling of guilt had receded to such an extent that she felt she could face my wrath. I am humbled to admit, I was shocked. I was shocked but I felt no wrath. I felt and I feel gratitude that we should have been blessed with such a neighbour who was willing to help; selflessly and without demand. Indeed, without questioning our beliefs and our traditions. We, too offer a toast to Meg, an exquisite example of a human. Thank you. We will hold you for ever in our hearts.'

Ted remembered how Meg had done some baby-sitting for the Almons. We argued about it because I thought she was feeling broody. Meg told me not to be so silly, she was already 45, way beyond wanting another baby crying all night and wanting attention all day. She never said there was a deeper meaning to the whole thing. I guess she realised how crushing it must have been for the Almons. Ah, Meg. A heart as big as a … 'To Meg,' he said.

'And to you, Mr Halloway,' added Sarah, 'we are here for you now. If ever you need anything, simply call. We have not and will not, forget the debt we owe your dear wife.'

Charles Riley said nothing. He was struggling himself. This was an area he needed to work on. The Jewish community were so restrictive towards others, there was no acceptance of necessity to communicate and interact with others. He was experiencing something new, he didn't know quite how to react.

He was aided by Chen Wang, who had realised that it was his turn to speak. All others were finished. He stood up and said, 'The white lilies here on this table are presented by my wife, Baihe, which is Chinese for Lily.

It is for her that I speak especially. We too, are a family concern. We have many members of our family and some also come to us regularly from home, in China. We need many workers to keep our restaurants and shops open. With the help of your dear wife, Mr Halloway, they feel more at home here. My wife, Baihe could speak no English when we arrived here so many years ago. And many more of our family members share this predicament. But your wife, Mr Halloway, she would help us learn. Your wife was always friendly to us and soon realised that Baihe could not be so friendly in return as her English was not so good. Their smiles became sentences and soon Baihe was going to your house almost every day to learn a little more English. Your dear wife would take no payment for her services so we were forced to stop it. Then the idea was born that we give our services to her in exchange. It was a perfect match.

She used our laundry and our take-away and we used her English to fill in forms and assist our family newcomers to England. Just as your wife continued to help our family when Baihe's English was good enough, so now we will continue to offer our services to you. May Meg be blessed in our memories. Thank you, Mr Halloway. We feel blessed to know you and your family.'

Ted suddenly remembered that Meg had sometimes helped some Chinese people with filling in forms. Gracious, he had never put two and two together before and he hadn't thought to question why she was doing it. What an afternoon this was turning out to be. He looked across at Ian, hoping he would pick up his unspoken message and stand up to say something on the family's behalf. Ted couldn't face it just yet. Unfortunately, Ian was obviously miles away – had he even been listening to all of this?

So, Ted simply said, 'Charles Riley, do tell us how you came to be in Empire Close, tell us of your ancestral roots. I'm sure everyone wants to know.'

Charles Riley was normally happy to take centre stage but felt uneasy doing so here, so he kept his story short.

He spoke of his research into his family background, his joy at finding the o'Donegal family and his grief at being too late to meet Michael o'Donegal in person. He told of the beauty of Monserrat and the destruction that befell it when the volcano erupted. Half of the island uninhabitable, his home and his lands destroyed. He spoke of the evacuation, of his son's journey to America and his travels to England. Who knows whether his daughter-in-law and grandchildren will remain with him here, or one day go to reunite with their father in Pennsylvania. One day, maybe he too will be alone in this wonderful house in this wonderful Close, for his wife too had died. Just ten months before the volcano did its worst, breast cancer had proved too strong an enemy for his beloved wife. With that, he sat down. He was finished with his tale – this was not his play, not his stage.

Ted was feeling way out of place. Imagine that, out of place in HIS Close. His mind was running amok. Time had come for him to take a serious look at himself. How long had he looked down on these people, felt they were not really quite up to scratch, not quite good enough to be living in Empire Close. My God, he thought, they were all foreigners, weren't they? At the start we were all true Brits, just wanting to get along with our lives. Then, slowly but surely, house by house, the Close changed hands. And now look at us. A group of – wonderful, interesting people.

Rosemary prodded her brother and whispered that it was time. He should say something to everyone, on behalf of the family.

So, he stood up and said, 'Neighbours, we are deeply touched by your stories. And deeply moved by the effort you all put in to arrange this Wake today. For this we owe you our sincerest thanks. Our mother (glanced towards Rosemary) and dad's wife (he didn't glance at Ted) was a special person, she was always there for us whenever we needed her, she always had time for us, always an open ear and always an open mind.

It is with great pride that I hear that you all know her in this way, as well. That she was able to give so much help and so much compassion to her neighbours – or should I say to her friends. I know I speak for my sister as well, when I say that we are somewhat uneasy at the thought of leaving our father to live alone now. As you all know, neither my sister nor I live close by, so it is particularly reassuring to know that my father is surrounded by so many friends and is in such good hands here in Empire Close. That he has so many looking out for him and willing to be there for him. For this we thank you from the bottom of our hearts.'

With this said, he sat down between his wife and his sister and turned to look at his father.

Ted was busy speaking to Charles Riley.

14
The House of Content

Ted, his children, and children-in-law returned to the house around 5:30 p. m. to find the grandchildren sat in front of the television. Ted offered everyone a drink – beers for the men, cola for the children and gin-and-tonic for the women. He told them they would have to get it themselves, due to his unfortunate situation but they were very welcome.

Rosemary waited for her father to leave the room and then approached Ian. 'What do you think? Shall we grown-ups go to the pub and have a chat?' 'Seems like an excellent idea to me,' answered her brother. They were both rather churned up by what they had heard and were more than just a little interested in what the other had to say. Rosemary was pensive but less worried than before about how her father would cope. She intended to speak to Dolly as soon as possible and to arrange for her to be a constant carer for Ted. He had the money; he could afford it and she was sure he wouldn't want to leave Empire Close in the very near future. She certainly wasn't intending to have him come and live with her, so she was eager to plot out a route forward as soon as possible. Ian on the other hand had not been worried about his father before and certainly wasn't about to start now. He had invested a minimal amount of grey matter on the subject of finances, considering just how much his father would be able to stem when it came to his day-to-day care but had quickly decided all would be OK. He was also of the opinion that, if all else failed, then Rosemary, as the daughter, would be the one to arrange for her father to move closer to her, be it into a residential home, or into her own home. After all he had heard from the neighbours, and all he had seen of his father's "new" attitude towards them, he was convinced that he would want to stay for as long as possible here in his established environment.

He did however have one big bundle hanging over his head – he was going to have to talk to Anita. He was only too aware of how she had experienced and perceived all that had happened and he could sense that she was itching to talk about the changes which would need to be made in their relationship. She had already, although they had barely been alone, made noises in such a direction. She seemed hell-bent on ensuring that he didn't turn into a clone of his father – after all these years, she wanted to change him! It was difficult for him, as it meant questioning himself but he caught himself contemplating if he really was too much like his father. And naturally, if that was such a bad thing. His father wasn't a bad person, he just had very old-fashioned views and was sometimes rather annoying, sometimes rather stubborn and sometimes, well slightly discriminating.

Ted settled himself in the study. He needed some time on his own, he had an awful lot to digest, it wasn't going to be easy. All he had heard; he should have known. It was entirely his fault that he didn't. Meg would never have lied to him – if he had asked what she had been doing all day, she would have told him. Or would she? He began to wonder if the reason she didn't say anything was that maybe she thought he would not approve. How could he not approve of her being such a wonderful person? Then it dawned on him that he had never really had much good to say when it came to the "second round" of neighbours they had. He had always prided himself in securing a family home in such a good neighbourhood, civilised was what he used to call it. He had been content in that environment. He had felt superior to the new neighbours; he was ashamed now to admit. Why, wasn't immigration the sincerest form of flattery? It was at this point that he realised he was still at it – still classing these people as immigrants. Forgetting that they were here by right and most of them already in the second generation.

He reflected on all their stories of where their parents and grandparents had come from – he recalled the emotion and the pride that had oozed through their words. They had all left something wonderful behind to come here and yet none seemed to be having second thoughts as to whether a good choice had been made. Great Britain – Empire Close – was their home.

Meg had never complained about their initial neighbours, but somehow she didn't seem to get as close to them as one might have thought normal. Ted smiled as he remembered how she had constantly tried to keep him away from Muriel Gemmell. Mary was an exception, of course, the two of them had hit it off right away – in spite of their husbands' initial scepticism. Ted had to smile again, funny that, isn't it? Where she was careful, I stepped in and where I was careful, she was busy helping out. What a team we were! And now look, with all her actions, she has ensured I will be well-accepted, well-cared for and well-admired in Empire Close. What a lovely bunch of neighbours I have – and so grateful and helpful.

Pity Michael wasn't here to share this with him. Oh, Michael – I am so sorry. Why did we have that fight? Damned Royals, that's what it was. When Diana was killed in that car crash and you proclaimed they were all but a privileged elitist pack and you provoked me into saying that I thought you were the personification of "plain living and high thinking", I didn't mean it harshly. I just meant you were well-read and didn't show-off. You stomped off to have a beer in your garden, where you claimed you would find peace. Two days later you found eternal peace. Gone from this world. I miss you, Michael.

Ted was distraught. He had lost two dear people and as coincidence would have it, he had not been able to say goodbye to either of them properly. Not only that – with Michael he had argued and with Meg he had been angry.

Ted now fought with himself. He felt he was being punished. Why should this be happening to him?

Meg was gone. They could no longer kiss-and-make-up. They could no longer even just hold each other and know all was forgiven.

Michael was gone. They could no longer share a beer and forget the world around them. They could no longer enjoy each other's company and know they could say anything, and all would be forgotten and forgiven the next day.

Ted realised that his children (and his grandchildren) would be returning home soon and they would, at least from a day-to-day, run-of-the mill perspective, be gone. He couldn't rely on them to be there when he needed help, or simply a chat.

He was alone now.

Although he did have Dolly, what a saint she was.

And he had Bernie and Daisy, what amiable people they were.

Not to mention, Charles Riley, the Nowaks, the Armatis, the Wangs and the Almons, that is. They were such kind people, who would believe it? Why, he had a mass of people to turn to! And they were all interesting and interested.

He was blessed indeed.

Michael had recited a poem to Ted once, written by an Irishman called James Clarence Mangan. He couldn't recall the whole poem but he could remember that it was about some poor soul who had been in search of all sorts of things throughout his life. For Ted, one part stood out and had remained with him over the years, "I rode in search of the House of Content but never could reach it, as far as I went. " Poor fellow, thought Ted and how lucky I count myself that that was not me. For, I found my House of Content, here in Empire Close with my Meg. And this House of Content may continue to be such, for it is well-founded on stone, chiselled into place by my Meg.

Another book by M.J. Boyle

"Mirror, Mirror on the Wall"
ISBN – 9781398428041